ON HIS BENDED KNEE

THE BRIDES OF PURPLE HEART RANCH BOOK 1

SHANAE JOHNSON

Edited by Alyssa Breck
Cover design by Ines Johnson

Manufactured in the United States of America
First Edition October 2018

CHAPTER ONE

T he sound of the hooves impacting the earth brought to mind the sound of artillery fire. It was a sound Dylan Banks knew all too well. He'd spent the last five years in a war zone. Any day during that time he might look up and see skies of azure blue, rolling hills of sand, or fields of pastel blooms. It was a cruel joke. War wasn't supposed to be pretty.

The sky was blue in this place. Farmland stretched out. The sound of the horses trotting and galloping wasn't the only thing reminding him of war. His men were there too. The ones that had made it out alive, anyway.

Those who escaped with their lives had lost many things. Family, friends, a part of their body, a part of their soul. But this place, the Bellflower Ranch, was healing them.

He looked over and caught the sigil of the ranch. It was a purple flower with rounded petals. The flower clearly resembled a heart. The veterans who now inhabited the sanctuary had taken to calling the ranch the Purple Heart Ranch, in honor of the scars and wounds they'd each brought home with them.

Dylan pushed his horse and himself to go faster. The sweet spring air hit his face. He pushed his body past what the doctors told him he was capable of doing. His hips had to work to absorb and control the movement of the horse. He felt the horse's powerful muscles stimulating his own, giving him the strength he needed to heal.

He hadn't believed healing was possible when he'd awakened in a military hospital and found himself no longer a whole man. But he was getting a part of himself back now on the Purple Heart Ranch. They all were.

This place had become a sanctuary for the wounded. A place where they wouldn't need to hide from their sleeping or waking nightmares. He hadn't been on good terms with God after his discharge. But when he had set foot on the ranch and climbed atop his first horse, he realized that God had given him a new purpose.

The military doctors had saved his life, but hippotherapy gave him his life back. The practice of using horseback riding as therapy for impaired movement had been what truly brought Dylan back to life after the war and his injuries.

He loved riding horses. He loved being on this ranch. He loved that he no longer had to take cover under a beautiful sky. After the hell that he and the other men had seen, the Purple Heart Ranch was the closest to heaven he'd ever get.

With a pull of the reins, Dylan urged the horse to a slow trot. They made their way back into the training area where Dylan dismounted. If he'd felt a pang of pain before, he felt a definite pounding as he lifted his thigh up and over the horse's back. The prosthetic stuck out like a sore thumb as he did so, and the muscles of his hips and thighs screamed.

The trainer, Mark, held back. He knew better than to offer a hand to the proud warriors. But he also knew when to ignore their pride and step in to give them extra care.

Although Dylan was sore, he didn't need the extra care today. He carefully lowered himself to the ground using mostly his upper body strength. He stood awkwardly for a moment until he had his bearings, and then he nodded to Mark.

The trainer only shook his head. He hadn't bothered arguing or offering commentary. But another man did.

"You went a little longer than you were supposed to, soldier."

Dylan stared Dr. Patel down. But even though Dylan had a good foot and a half on the older man, Dr. Patel still had a commanding presence. He smiled, but his eyes were stern and sharp, missing nothing. His voice was chiding, but at the same time paternal with the lilting accent of his homeland of India.

"I can take it," Dylan said as he moved toward the man. He tried to hide his grimace as his prosthetic leg tried to buckle.

Dylan knew he hadn't fooled the psychologist who watched him with a raised brow. "Just because you can take it doesn't mean you should."

The older man moved closer, but like Mark, Dr. Patel knew better than to offer assistance unless absolutely necessary. Dylan made sure it was never necessary. The problem didn't require a hand, just a readjustment of his load.

The socket of his prosthetic had likely loosened.

He stood still and bared down, pushing his stump until he heard the telltale clicks of the socket reconnecting with the liner.

"The old ball and chain and I are getting along fine," said Dylan as he straightened to his natural height. The prosthetic leg gave him an extra inch. That was a benefit, at least.

"Your body is healing," said Dr. Patel. "All of the men here are doing well in body. But you also have to heal your hearts. Love heals the internal wounds."

Dylan had heard this speech from the man before. He'd agreed to the therapy for his mind. After all he'd been through, he recognized that he needed someone to talk to about the horrors of combat. But he didn't like it when the good doctor aimed for the heart.

"Maybe you should get your family up here?" Dr. Patel suggested.

Dylan shook his head. He had no desire to see his family. And they'd made it clear that, now that he was half a man, they were just fine without him.

"Or maybe leave the ranch for a date?" offered Dr. Patel.

None of the veterans staying at the ranch left for dates. Well, except for Xavier Ramos. Ramos still had all his limbs and his looks. The women he went out with never saw his wound unless he took off his clothes.

"Although, I'm still skeptical about dating with phone apps and computer programs," said Dr. Patel. "In my country, we trusted our elders to find us life-partners."

Dylan had met Mrs. Patel a number of times. It warmed his heart whenever he saw the couple together. They each took such care with one another, offering secret smiles, and fussing over tiny things.

Dylan had always imagined himself so fortunate. But the woman he'd given his ring to had handed it back before he'd even left the hospital. His injury hadn't allowed him to go after her. His pride would not have let him. His heart hadn't made it a priority.

"I'm not looking for love right now," Dylan said. He conveniently left off the words *at all*.

He wouldn't be looking for love ever again. If his own family couldn't love him, if his fiancée left him after she'd seen what he'd become, how could a stranger ever love the man he would be for the rest of his days.

"That's the thing about arranged marriage," said Dr. Patel. "You get the partner first. Love comes in time."

"Are you ready to start our session?" Dylan asked, pointing the way to Dr. Patel's office to get him on a different track. "I've been having some nightmares."

Unlike some of the other vets on the ranch, Dylan never had nightmares. His sleep was dreamless and dark.

Once again, Dr. Patel wasn't fooled, but he let Dylan lead him to his office. Dylan knew the old man meant well, but this wasn't a road he wanted to go down. He'd been hurt enough in this life.

CHAPTER TWO

Maggie looked down at the sleeping animal on the surgery table. The bright lights of the surgical theater illuminated the room, casting no shadows on her performance. The blade in her hand wasn't working its normal magic, and she had no more tricks up her sleeve. The dog would lose both its hind legs.

Though the dog was asleep, his lower lip trembled as though he knew what was about to happen to him. It looked as though he was trying to keep a stiff upper lip in the face of adversity. She, of all people, understood that. Life had beaten the little guy up and spit him back out to deal with it on his own.

He had no tags. No collar. He'd been left on the

doorstep of the veterinary clinic sometime in the early morning. Maggie had arrived to see the animal bleeding on the pristine steps. He'd eyed her warily, too tired to snarl. His eyes had simply closed in resignation while he waited for her to try and do worse to him. What she did was scoop him up and set down to work.

The dog could tell Maggie's own life story. Though she'd never been physically beaten, she'd taken more than her share of emotional hits. She'd been abandoned by her parents while in elementary school. Literally, while she was in elementary school. They had simply left her there and never picked her up.

She'd gone into the foster system to wait them out. They never came back.

At first, she took it as her due. She knew that many animals abandoned their children at young ages. But that reasoning hadn't stuck long as she continued to see parents picking up their kids from school, loading them in their car, and taking them home. She watched as siblings and kids from the same neighborhood or kids with the same interest formed packs and stuck together, preying on anyone who was a lone kid.

Maggie was alone. The other kids in the foster

system either hadn't accepted her into their group or they got adopted and never came back. Maggie had never had a pack; not a human one at least.

No adult had ever advocated for her. She'd been left to rot in the system, never finding a family to adopt her as their own. She'd been fostered, another word for used for a paycheck or cheap labor, until she came of age and picked herself up and out of the vicious cycle.

But this poor dog could no longer stand on its own four feet due to its injury. It would never run again. No one would want a disabled dog. It had no one to stick up for him and now it would be put down permanently.

Maggie put down the blade and picked up the needle filled with blue juice. The pentobarbital would be a mercy to the poor creature. She knew that. She'd seen countless cases that began with a different wound or illness and ended up right back here on this table, under these lights, in the middle of a surgical theater with no one watching or caring about the show.

"Maggie, let's hurry this up. I have a 2 pm tee time on the golf course."

Dr. Art Cooper was the owner of the theater Maggie was currently performing in. He had a script for times like these, and the story always ended the same way.

"Just prick the mutt already so I can close shop." He said the words without glancing up at her or the animal at the end of his life.

A sound on the other side of the door had Dr. Cooper glancing up. He slipped on his interested face as one of the new vet nurses walked by. Of course, he smiled at her. He had to keep up the facade that he was a decent human being.

A second later, his interested face turned over to his excited face as a client presented her ancient, smelly, arthritic cat to him. She was a very good client; coming for every screening he suggested, buying the most expensive brand of pet food that he was pushing that month, and always ready to take a look at the newest pet insurance offerings. The moment the cat lady and her cat were gone, the animated expression melted off his face and was replaced with disgust.

Maggie hated the man. How could anyone work with animals and have no care for them? They were all nothing but a paycheck to him. As a vet tech, she had the luxury of not making enough to be so callous.

She really had no luxuries at all. Definitely not

enough to care for another wounded animal. Maggie looked down on the table at the sleeping dog. A single tear slid down his cheek, and the floodgates opened.

Maggie looked up at Dr. Cooper and painted on a smile to rival his performance. "Why don't you go ahead and head out. I can take care of this and close up shop for you."

Dr. Cooper eyed her suspiciously. Then he looked down at the dog. "We're not going to have another problem, are we? You've already had one strike, another and I'll let you go."

That was one thing about being a doctor, they were some of the smartest people. The last time Maggie had been asked to put a dog down, she'd snuck him out the back door of the clinic. He was now resting comfortably in her home. Probably in her closet on a pile of her shoes.

"This animal won't have any quality of life," Dr. Cooper was saying. "It would take hundreds of dollars a month to maintain him."

Wasn't a single life worth that, she wanted to say. But she hadn't. Instead, she told the truth. "I understand. I've learned my lesson. I need this job to take care of the animals I do have."

She had four dogs, all of whom had severe

injuries and illnesses that cost her more than her rent to care for. If she lost this job, she wouldn't have the money to care for them or keep a roof over her head.

Maggie picked up the needle and gave it a few flicks with her index finger.

Dr. Cooper looked at the time. Then he looked back at her. His tee time won out like she knew it would. He turned in his expensive gator boots and walked out the door.

Maggie breathed a sigh of relief and put the needle down. She bandaged the dog. The damage had been done long before she'd gotten to him and healing had already begun. Now she just needed to heal his spirit alongside his body.

Maggie wrapped the dog up in a blanket, and she made her way to the back. She was nearly out of the door when she rounded a corner. Dr. Cooper looked up from his watch at her. And of course, that's when the dog decided to wake up from his meds and bark.

It was a low, groggy bark that she might have been able to play off as her own stomach grumbling. She had missed lunch again. But the trickle of liquid that streamed out of the blanket and onto Dr. Cooper's expensive boots, she had no excuse for. In fact, she was quite pleased by it.

The little dog was a good boy. She wasn't sure how she'd feed and care for him now that she was out of a job, but she was keeping him.

CHAPTER THREE

Dylan headed back to the stables after his session with Dr. Patel. The good doctor hadn't pushed him on the fake nightmares. He hadn't exactly pursued the discussion of dating either. What he'd done was far worse. He'd engaged Dylan in a chat about his broken engagement.

Hilary Weston had been the girl next door. But next door had been one floor down from the penthouse of one of the most exclusive residential buildings in New York City. Living his life on top of her, watching her preen beneath him, it was inevitable that one day she'd end up on his arm.

Hilary had been Dylan's first everything. His first crush. His first girlfriend. His first ... everything.

She hadn't been happy when he announced he

wanted to go into the military. With his family money and his trust fund, Dylan could've sat on his laurels for a few lifetimes over. But he'd felt called.

He'd left with promises to do only one tour and then come back for a wedding as grand as she wanted to make it. They'd joked that it would take her the duration of his tour to plan the social event of the decade. But when Dylan returned covered in bruises and missing a limb, Hilary made other plans.

It hadn't mattered to her that he could've taken care of her financially, she was an heiress in her own right. It hadn't mattered to her that he was a war hero. She was a society darling, constantly in the gossip pages. Appearances mattered to Hilary Weston, and having a wounded warrior covered in bruises and missing a limb was not a good look.

She'd let the door slam behind her as she walked out of the military hospital room. She'd gotten engaged to another man and married him all within the last six months. Dylan heard the guy was some type of reality star, and now Hilary was too.

He'd liked to think he'd dodged a bullet. But he'd dodged them in real life. Her rejection stung.

But that life was over. This was his new reality now. And it was one he thrived in.

Dylan turned from his sour memories and

looked around the ranch. He'd given up high society living for mucking out stalls and tilling the earth. It was the best decision of his life.

The ranch had been fledgling before he infused it with what amounted to a small portion of his inheritance. His parents had balked at the idea until they realized their deformed son would be safely tucked away out of society's and their eyes. Like Hilary, the Banks were all about keeping up appearances. A decorated soldier serving his country looked good. An amputee hobbling about did not.

For the second time today, the sound of hooves reminded him of artillery fire. But Dylan didn't suffer from PTSD in the normal sense. It was just the trauma of his family that affected him. So, when he saw Sean Jeffries riding at a trot, he could only smile up at the man.

Jeffries had come home from war with all his limbs. But like all the men on the ranch, Jeffries had left a piece of himself behind in the war zone. Jeffries dipped his head in greeting, pulling his cowboy hat low over his brown forehead. Dark shades covered his face. The sunglasses cast the dark man on the steed in a full shadow. Jeffries didn't like people looking at the scars on his face.

Still, Jeffries held his posture erect and his head

high. Life looked differently from on top of a horse. Not only did the therapy help improve physical injuries, it also helped improve balance, control, and coordination of the mind. Having control of a great beast and regaining control of one's self increased self-esteem and gave a sense of freedom.

The ranch didn't just offer horse therapy. Gardening helped with sensory and tactile functions. Chores like pushing a wheelbarrow, raking, hoeing, weeding, planting and even arranging flowers all built or rebuilt motor skills.

Reed Cannon was on his knees in the gardens. Cannon moved aside the dirt and planted flowers, evenly spacing them out. The fingers of one hand worked in the fertile soil, while the others remained stiff against the dirt. The stiff hand was a prosthetic. He'd lost the real one in the same explosion that took Dylan's leg.

Dylan walked on through the haven, passing by the purple bellflowers for which the ranch was named. There weren't just the flower and vegetable gardens in this sanctuary. There was also a butterfly garden that offered the vets peace and tranquility. This place was not just for healing mentally and physically, but also emotionally. Dylan and the others had lain down wheelchair paths to make it accessible for all.

Older veterans came to the ranch for help as well, getting care for wars long past but whose scars were still fresh. Someday Dylan hoped they would be able to open up the ranch to troubled youth and give them the care they needed to have a chance at a bright future. So no, he didn't bemoan leaving high society behind. This was the society he wanted to create.

As Dylan came away from the gardens, the smell of livestock hit his nose. Francisco DeMonti moved amongst the sheep. The care of small animals helped the men to learn to once more form relationships with others. Animals were the perfect specimens. Many offered unconditional love, especially if there was food in your outstretched hand.

Fran had no visible scars. His wounds were all internal, and they still had a good chance of killing him.

"Good ride this morning?" asked Fran as he came out of the enclosure and joined Dylan on the path toward the main buildings.

Dylan nodded.

"Got a call from an old buddy at the vet center,"

said Fran. "They're wondering if we could house a couple more soldiers?"

"We've got the space."

There were living quarters on the ranch. Though most soldiers didn't stay after their therapy or rehab was complete. Many had families to return to, or they found that long-term ranch life didn't agree with them. The five vets who made the ranch their home didn't have that luxury or didn't want to go back to it. For them, this was home now.

"We'll take anyone that needs the help," said Dylan.

And they could at little to no cost. Between their pensions, which Dylan refused to let anyone spend, the government aide, which Dylan put to giving all the workers a pay increase, and Dylan's trust fund, which took on the bulk of the expenses, they would never need to turn anyone away. Unlike how his family treated him.

"Have a good evening boys," called Dr. Patel. The man headed to his car with his briefcase in one hand and a Bible in the other. In addition to being a licensed psychologist, he was also a man of the cloth.

"Headed to church?" asked Fran.

"That I am." Dr. Patel smiled. "There's room in the passenger seat if you'd like to accompany me."

"Another time," said Fran.

Dylan remained mute. He still hadn't healed his relationship with the man upstairs, and he wasn't quite ready to start now. But Dr. Patel simply smiled that knowing smile at both of them. If Dylan didn't respect the man as much as he did, he'd be annoyed at his universal upbeat attitude, perpetual patience in the face of adversity, and consistent certainty in all things.

As Dr. Patel pulled his car door open, another car pulled up. It was an expensive luxury model. For a moment, Dylan wondered if it was his father. But he knew his father would never leave Manhattan to come out into the middle of nowhere America.

The man who stepped out of the car wore an expensive suit. The ensemble was off the rack and not tailor-made. His father would never be caught dead in something that wasn't crafted especially for him. Dylan recognized the man as Michael Haskell, the land agent for the ranch.

Haskell was no-nonsense and to the point. He didn't fuss around with niceties and unimportant details. Dylan had been leasing the land for nearly a year waiting for the sale to go through. There were only a few minor details left before the deed was in Dylan's hand.

"We got a problem," said Haskell. "The land was originally designated for family use. The sale won't go through unless there are families here."

"This unit of soldiers is a family," said Dylan.

"This unit is a group of men," said Haskell. "None of whom are married."

Dylan couldn't understand how this was a problem? He was buying land not an amusement park. What did it matter who lived on the land?

"How do we fix this?" asked Fran, ever the practical one. "Can we get the zoning changed?"

"It'll take months to get the zoning changed, and you'll need to vacate while you do," said Haskell. "I don't suppose any of you are getting married anytime soon?"

CHAPTER FOUR

"I let you get away with two dogs when the rules clearly state one small dog. Over the past two years, you've accumulated four dogs and only two of them are small."

Maggie cradled one of the small dogs in her arms as her landlord spoke. Soldier had lost her front paw after being hit by a car. She'd been brought into the vet clinic during Maggie's first month there. She'd been able to heal Soldier, amputating her mangled leg and teaching her to walk on three legs. The little dog thrived, but no one came to claim her nor welcome her into a new home. She was slated for being put down, but somehow she'd magically disappeared before her date with death.

Maggie put Soldier down on the hardwood floor

of the entryway. Her nails clinked as she sauntered across the floor, clearly not enjoying Mr. Hurley's company any more than he was enjoying hers.

The three other dogs Mr. Hurley referred to kept their distance. They were typically a very loving bunch, eager to greet new people and make a new human friend when anyone came to the door or they were out in public. But they instinctively knew that Mr. Hurley was not the buddy type.

"And now you're adding a fifth?" demanded Mr. Hurley.

The fifth dog cowered beneath her coffee table. He'd recovered nicely from his surgery and had been up and curious the next day. Maggie had fitted him with a doggie wheelchair that she'd fashioned herself. It took the dog just one day to master the apparatus and now he was flying around her small apartment. Maggie had named him Spin.

Maggie went over and picked up Spin. Then she turned and faced her landlord with her most winningest smile. It was all she could afford since she no longer had a job to pay rent. She hoped the little Irish Terrier's sweet face would win over Mr. Hurley.

"They've never caused you any trouble," she said as she nuzzled the side of Spin's face. The dog gave her an appreciative lick, then hid his head beneath her chin. "You barely know they're here."

Her dogs didn't bark much. Maggie guessed that they'd learned that raising their voices could lead to a strike from a human. So, they were mostly quiet.

She didn't mention that Stevie, her partially blind Rottweiler, had scratched up the cabinets in the bathroom. Or that Sugar, her diabetic Golden Retriever, had thrown up in the bedroom so many times that Maggie had lost her ability to be nose-blind to it.

But it wasn't necessary. Mr. Hurley was unmoved by any of their puppy dog eyes. "That's beside the point. You're breaking the rules. I would've let it go with two dogs, but not five. Unless you can follow the rules and have only one small dog, you'll need to find a new place to live."

"You can't be serious? I can't choose between my dogs."

"Find them a good home with other families."

That hadn't worked the first time. That's why they were all there. Most single professionals and families with children weren't interested in taking in an older or wounded animal. They all wanted puppies just out of the womb who would run around on all four feet and have enough energy to catch a ball.

And she knew from experience that she couldn't put the dogs in a shelter while she found a new home. They'd be put down before the end of the week. That is, if she could even get a new job to put a roof over their heads, food in their bowls, and medicine in their bodies.

What was she going to do?

Mr. Hurley walked away without another word, deaf to her protests.

That was a blow. One she had known was possible. She had been breaking the rules for quite some time. But she hadn't thought he'd actually throw her out. Now she saw that her time was up. She had no job and now would have no place to live.

But she wasn't giving up. She never gave up. No matter how bleak the situation. There was always a way.

One by one, Maggie piled the dogs into the back of her truck. She had to put the dogs in crates while she drove so that they wouldn't injure themselves any further. Soldier, the Chihuahua, Star, the Pug, and Spin went into the back. Spin was not at all happy about being confined and immediately began to cry. Maggie took a moment to soothe him with a chew toy, then she piled Sugar, the retriever, into the back front seat and guided Stevie, her partially blind Rottweiler, into the back.

With the gang all loaded up, she started the car and headed to the only place she could think of. Church. She needed a miracle to get herself out of this one.

The church was tucked in the back corner of the city, as though it were a secret. But the congregation was a healthy size, had always been since Maggie had started going there as a teenager. Next to the church sat the cold, gray group home that Maggie had spent most of her youth in. It was a drabby, unattractive sister next to the red brick and white trim of the church.

The church was the place Maggie had found solace on her bleak nights. She'd prayed to God to bring her parents back to her. When those prayers went unanswered, she'd prayed for a new mom and dad to love her. Even when those prayers hadn't been answered as she'd hoped, Maggie never gave up because at some point while she was on her knees in the pews, she looked around to realize that the people of the church had become her family.

Maggie pulled into the parking lot near the back of the church. One by one, she took her dogs out and walked them to the grassy yard where many a summer picnic had been held. Pastor David was a dog lover. He and Maggie had bonded over their love of animals when she was young. She'd hoped that Pastor David would adopt her, but he was unmarried and had remained so all his life. Still, he always left the door open for her. And that policy of open doors continued even after his death.

"There's my favorite veterinarian."

Maggie turned at the sound of the familiar voice. Her smile was big and her arms opened wide before she saw Pastor Patel.

"There's my favorite shrink."

The two embraced. As the embrace ended, Maggie gave the man an extra squeeze. It had been too long since she'd been held, and she needed the care today.

Pastor Patel pulled away but kept a hold of her. He didn't ask any questions. Just cocked his head, looking down at her with those light brown eyes and waited.

"I'm fine." She waved his concern away, but the tears had already formed in her eyes.

Maggie never cried. As a foster child living in the group home, she knew it was pointless. She wouldn't get any extra care. When she was placed in a foster home, she knew it was pointless. Her foster parents had no care for her, only that she was another paycheck for them and that she was old enough to care for the rest of their fostered brood.

But, like Pastor David, Pastor Patel had always cared for her. And he was always able to get her to divulge her feelings.

"I've just had the worst week," she said. As though he heard her talking about him, Spin came up to her leg, wheel coming to a halt as he looked up at her apologetically.

"I see you have a new pack member." Pastor Patel bent down and offered the back of his hand to Spin. Spin gave the hand a sniff. Then a lick. Then a bob of his head, as if recognizing that Pastor Patel was good people.

Maggie gave a sniff of her own and then it all came out in a rush. "They wanted me to put him down because he was injured. When I said no, they let me go. And now my landlord says I have to get rid of four of them if I want to keep my place. How can people be so cruel? They're my family. Just because they're wounded doesn't mean they don't deserve love."

Pastor Patel looked down at her. His eyes always made her think of a serene Buddha statue. She knew he'd seen all of that before she'd said a single word. "Quite right, my dear. A wounded animal is best healed by love."

"I didn't know where else to turn," said Maggie. "I was hoping for a miracle."

Dr. Patel nodded, eyes sparkling with some revelation. "I think I might be able to help."

CHAPTER FIVE

"Wives? As in married? To women?"

"Unless there's something about you that we should know, Ramos."

Xavier Ramos reached over and tried to smack Reed Cannon in the head, but the other man raised his prosthetic arm to ward off the attack. There was nothing wrong with his reflexes. Ramos's flesh hit Cannon's metal and Ramos winced.

"Can't we get the zoning changed?" asked Sean Jeffries. He had his sunglasses off now that they were all inside one of the ranch's barns.

The men had converted the old barn into a gaming room complete with large flat screens, an old-fashioned record player and tape deck, and every gaming console including an antique Atari which Rees had brought back to life with his techno-genius.

"It would be a long process," said Dylan. "And in the meantime, we'd all have to leave the ranch while the powers that be waded through all the red tape."

The men were lounging in recliners or sitting on bar stools, but an anxious hum went around the room. The ranch was their haven, their home. Even for those who had somewhere that they could go, leaving was not an option.

Unlike with Dylan, Jeffries's family hadn't rejected him. They called the ranch on a regular basis. It was Jeffries who didn't want them to see him. It wasn't just the scar on his face that shamed him. He suffered from PTSD and was prone to flash-backs. He could be taken back to the war-torn deserts of the Middle East when he slept, or with loud noises he could readily identify. The men surrounding him knew how to manage his episodes. But Jeffries was terrified of hurting someone he cared about. And so he stayed away from his family and wouldn't receive their calls.

"Aren't you all missing the obvious?" They all turned to Reed and waited for his revelation. Reed took his time. The man had a bit of the flare for the dramatic at times. "We just need to get married."

Eyes and heads rolled as everyone turned away from the proclamation. Except Fran.

"It's not a bad idea," Fran said. "People do it all the time. For green cards, for financial stability, some fools even do it for something called love."

Dylan had been such a fool who wanted to get married for love. Or what he thought was love. He had no idea where the plan came from as his own parents hadn't been in love.

Catherine and Charles Banks had married for social standing. The irony was that they couldn't stand each other. Though the rest of society would never know it. At parties, they put on a show of devotion and compatibility. They used to put on the show at home for Dylan when he was a kid. But they soon stopped caring about what he saw behind the closed doors of their many homes, which they often occupied separately.

"Who would want to marry a bunch of broken soldiers?" asked Sean.

"Hey, we're not broken." Dylan almost believed the words coming out of his own mouth. "We served our country. We are highly skilled. We are loyal, dedicated men."

Though the speech was impassioned, the faces around him looked doubtful.

"Frances might have a point," said Xavier, using the feminization of the name to get under Fran's skin like they all did from time to time. "There are a lot of hard-up women out there. Some probably need a place to stay, money in their pocket, or just a good lay."

Now it was Dylan who rolled his eyes and neck at the preposterous direction the discussion was taking. He needed his men to focus on viable solutions to this very real problem. But the other men were listening to Xavier's nonsense.

"Dr. Patel is always saying we need a good woman to heal our hearts." Reed picked up the gauntlet of the insanity. He was a romantic at heart and still believed love was waiting to come into his arms. "Maybe now's the time."

"Patel had an arranged marriage," said Fran. "And it worked for him."

"This is the Wild West," said Reed. "This kind of stuff happened here all the time. Remember the Gold Rush Brides?"

"That was California," Sean said. The man was a walking encyclopedia. "You mean mail order brides."

"It would be email now," said Fran. "No one uses the postal system."

"We are not finding women on Craig's List," said Dylan, pinching the bridge of his nose and squeezing his eyes shut in exasperation.

"Then how are we gonna stay here?"

Dylan wasn't sure which man said it, but he knew they all were thinking it. He opened his eyes and faced the room full of men. They'd looked to him for leadership when they were in combat, and they looked at him the same way now. How would they win this particular war on the home front?

"We'll petition the court," said Dylan. "I have a few contacts in the government."

"We have more recruits coming in a couple of month. What are we gonna do with them?"

Dylan didn't have an answer for that. He didn't know how he would take in another wounded soldier only to potentially turn the man away. As he prepared to turn around, a flash of fur ran through the room.

No, ran wasn't exactly the right word. Two front paws ran. The two back paws were not there. Instead, two wheels acted as legs that the little dog used to propel himself onward.

Dylan wasn't the only one who spotted the animal. The other soldiers turned and stared at the creature. The dog stared back. It also slowed down as it looked up at all the big humans eying it.

The dog had had a grin on his face, but under the close scrutiny, his muzzle closed. He pulled his lolling tongue back into his mouth and let out a low whimper.

Dylan bent down to be on the dog's level. He rested on his good knee, which was a difficult feat for him after a long day. But he had to get a closer look at this dog and his apparatus.

The dog made a slow beeline for Dylan. Dylan put his hand out to the dog. The dog gave the back of his hand a tentative sniff and then a lick.

Who would do such a thing as to take a dog's hind legs? But more importantly, who would take the time to make a contraption that gave the animal back a semblance of the life he once knew?

"I'm so sorry," said a feminine voice. "That's my dog."

Dylan looked up into the face of the woman. She was dressed in a T-shirt and jeans. Her hair was pulled back in a messy ponytail. She wasn't wearing a lick of makeup. She looked fresh, clean, capable.

She marched into the room, not like she was on a

catwalk, but like she was on a mission. She reached for the dog and he saw her hands were un-manicured. When one of her rough fingers brushed the skin of his forearm, Dylan felt a spark. His breath caught and so did hers.

CHAPTER SIX

Dazzling.

That was the only word Maggie could use to describe the blue of his eyes. They weren't crystal clear because there was a hint of navy. But the color was a little too light to be categorized as exactly navy. So, dazzling it was.

And he was staring at her. No, not staring. Gazing.

Maggie knew the difference. She'd had plenty of people stare at her in elementary school when they discovered that Santa had never come to her house. Or when she wore outdated hand-me-downs in middle school. Or when she temporarily went vegan in high school. Or when she insisted she could save an animal that was clearly bound for pet heaven.

Those were all stares that said, "What is with this girl?," or "Would you look at this poor thing," or "What an annoying woman."

None of those was the look coming from the dazzling blue eyes gazing down at her. That look was one of curiosity. It was a look of surprise. Was it a look of ... interest?

No. That couldn't be right. A man that beautiful, with dazzling eyes like those, and a strong square chin, and blond hair that settled in perfect waves, wouldn't be interested in a girl like her.

Maggie was plain, where he was perfect. She was slight, where he was fit and toned. She was not unattractive per say, where he was drop-dead gorgeous.

Then she realized, that gaze wasn't meant for her. He'd lifted his gaze from Spin to her. That curiosity, that surprise, that interest, it had to be for Spin and his apparatus. She was just receiving the residual effects of him looking at her dog.

Still, that was a huge mark in the man's favor. He'd shown compassion and kindness to a dog, a wounded one at that. The man had scooped Spin, apparatus and all, up into his strong embrace.

Spin was happily wagging his tail in the man's arms. The dog's tongue lolled as he panted happily and gave the man pure puppy dog eyes. Spin whimpered when Maggie tried to take him back. And that's when she felt it.

Though Maggie had little to no experience with men, she was a red-blooded woman. She knew what the spark was. That's what she felt when her fingertips touched the big, gazing, dazzling man.

The spark wasn't hot like a fire. It was like Fourth of July sparklers being set off all over her skin. She wanted to shiver, but she felt too warm.

"This is your dog?" he asked.

If his skin was like sparklers, his voice was like honey; golden and smooth with just the right amount of sweetness. It took Maggie a moment to find her voice. Even after a moment of searching, her voice still wouldn't come out of hiding. So, she simply nodded.

The man stretched out his muscled arms to hand Spin over, but the dog again whimpered. Spin was cradled back in the man's arms looking doubtfully at Maggie.

"We're new to each other," she said. "We only just met a few days ago when I rescued him."

"Rescued him?" The man took one hand and rubbed Spin's head. The dog preened at the attention.

"I rescued Spin here from my boss. He wanted me to kill him."

Low growls went up through the room. Maggie turned to see that she was in a room full of equally big and beautiful men. But she didn't feel an ounce of fear. She was a good judge of character when it came to danger. She got the sense that any of these men would stand up to defend the weak.

"I'm a vet tech," she said. "Or at least I was. My boss, the veterinarian, wanted me to put him down because he felt it was a kindness with his injury."

The mood changed in the room. She could tell she was in a room of people who strongly disagreed with Dr. Cooper's prognosis.

"Instead, I patched him up and dognapped him."

"Atta girl," someone called.

"Yeah, well, I lost my job because of it," she said. "That's why I'm here. I'm looking for Pastor—I mean, Dr. Patel. He said there might be a place for me here?"

"A place for you here?" The man who held her dog repeated her words.

Maggie nodded. "Yeah, he said it would include room and board and a place for my animals, as well. I just got kicked out of my apartment for having too many dogs. So, I'm hoping this job pans out because it's all I've got."

Heads turned to and fro. The men all looked at each other as though they shared an inside joke. Only, no one was laughing.

CHAPTER SEVEN

Dylan learned that the woman's name was
Maggie. The name suited her somehow. It
was a strong sound with just the right amount of
femininity.

They all filed into Dr. Patel's office. And by *they*
he meant himself, Spin the dog who'd burst into the
barn, Maggie, and her dog Soldier, whom she said
didn't do well with new people. Her other three dogs
were outside checking out their new surroundings
under the watchful eyes of the other soldiers.

The Rottweiler with a gash over his eye had
given one sniff to Sean's leg and began trailing
blindly after him. Sean gave the dog a scratch
behind the ears and walked slowly so the partially
blind dog could keep up.

The Pug, with star-like patches missing from his back, and the overweight Retriever began a sorry looking game of catch with two of the other soldiers. Reed tossed a ball with his good arm. The dogs sauntered after it. Then stared down at it instead of picking it up. Finally, Fran picked up the ball and tried again. With the same effect.

Xavier held back. He'd introduced himself to Maggie with a cocky grin and a wink. But when Maggie took the rest of her dogs out of her truck, Dylan wasn't surprised when Xavier took a few steps back. He'd once been a dog person, but that was before he'd lost not one, but two war dogs.

Dylan held the door for Maggie and then waited for her to sit down with the Chihuahua in her lap before he settled with Spin who still refused to be parted from him. He couldn't help but notice that the little dog was missing a front paw. Like Spin, the little dog had an enhancement to help it get around. It seemed all of Maggie's animals were wounded in some light.

Dylan looked up at Dr. Patel, suspicion etched in the grooves on his forehead. But as always, the man smiled a patient, wise smile. The Chihuahua jumped down from Maggie's arms and wagged his tail until Dr. Patel picked her up and settled her onto his lap.

"So, Maggie, I see you've met Dylan."

Maggie turned and smiled at Dylan. Once again, Dylan felt a spark of something in his chest, something he thought long snuffed. He had the urge to lean across his chair and sniff her like Spin was doing to him. He held back from the insane urge, cradling the dog in his arms as a barrier.

"I have," Maggie said as she faced him. "Are you the one in charge here? I'm sorry, I didn't dress formally or bring in my resume. I didn't realize the job interview would be today."

"Job interview?" Dylan turned to Dr. Patel.

"Like I told you in the barn, I'm a vet tech," Maggie said. "Pastor Patel led me to believe you needed help here on the ranch? I was coming by to check it out."

"Oh, Dylan needs help," said Dr. Patel. "But it's a different type of job."

Dylan could feel his face growing hot. He felt a phantom ache in his knee that was no longer there.

"What kind of job?" asked Maggie, still oblivious to Dr. Patel's machinations.

"A permanent one," said Dr. Patel. "The two of you have a lot in common. Commonalities make for strong relationship bonds."

"If you're suggesting what I think you're suggesting, then just stop," said Dylan. But he knew better. Dr. Patel always pushed the issue in that gentle, unassuming way of his.

"Maggie is a good girl; a kind soul that only looks to help others. You're the same. She just lost her home, and so have all of these animals. You're about to lose your home, and so will all of the soldiers here. If the two of you joined forces, each of you could come away with what you want, and perhaps more than you were expecting."

"I don't understand?" said Maggie.

Dylan couldn't stand for Dr. Patel to say it in that patient, rational way of his. The idea was certifiably insane, and the tone and the word choice needed to emphasize that. "He has the crazy idea that we should get married."

He waited for a breath before he turned to face her. Maggie's face was screwed in confusion. She turned in her chair and looked Dylan up and down. Dylan held still, feeling as though he were caught in the crosshairs of a sniper rifle as Maggie beheld him. Her verdict had to be that she found him wanting because she leaned back.

Dylan didn't listen as Dr. Patel further explained the predicament they found themselves in and the benefits of his solution. Dylan turned his focus on the dog.

Spin looked up at him with sad eyes. His front paws scratched at Dylan's heart. Spin's mouth split into a hopeful grin, like a divorced kid who wanted a new daddy.

Dylan gave the dog a scratch behind the ears, and the dog sighed, grateful for the attention. It was all he could do. He wouldn't become this dog's daddy.

"You can't be serious," Maggie was saying.

She was pretty, with a good heart, and smart. She might take in wounded dogs, but wounded men were a different story. Dylan had always imagined being married and having children. But that door was closed to him now. He couldn't be a father to a child in his condition. He couldn't be a husband to a wife either.

He had to admit that he found Maggie attractive. She was unassumingly pretty. Not like the society girls he was used to. She was the girl next door, but from a different neighborhood. It probably took her a few minutes to get ready in the morning, and the little effort is what made her stunning.

Her face was fresh and clean. Her scent earthy and not expensive and cloying. She didn't cross her legs at the ankle as she sat. Both of her hiking boots were planted firmly on the ground. There had been an animal resting in her lap. Now that her lap was vacant, she rested her elbows on her knees as she leaned forward listening intently to Dr. Patel.

No, she was not Dylan's type. The only reason he felt any attraction to her had to be because it had been so long since he'd been with a woman. So long since he'd even been around an available woman. But none of those old dreams were available to him.

"Maggie," Dr. Patel was saying, "you told me yourself, you have nowhere to go. And you have little money. No place you could afford would allow you to take all your dogs. You'll have to take them to the pound, and you, of all people, know what would happen to them."

Maggie chewed at her lower lip, at the same time twisting the corner between her thumb and forefinger. Dylan couldn't take his eyes off the movement of her fingers and tooth. He felt himself panting like the dog in his arms.

"I know you haven't had any luck at love," Dr. Patel said. "Dylan's a good man, an honorable man. And like I said, the two of you are a match. My gut tells me so. The two of you would suit if you give it a chance."

Maggie's cheeks had flamed as Dr. Patel talked about her love life or lack thereof. Want dropped in Dylan's belly, so heavy his gut grumbled.

"He does have a point," said Dylan.

Maggie lifted her gaze to him. The color slowly drained from her cheeks as she did so. Her gaze was uncertain, wary, as though she was expecting to hear the punchline of a bad joke at any second. But Dylan wasn't joking. A strategic plan was forming in his mind.

"We could give it a trial period," he said. "You can stay here, with your dogs, of course. We could use a hand with the farm animals. You can earn some extra money, have a roof over your head. And if it doesn't work out in thirty days, if we find we don't click, you'll have some extra cash and the time to look for someplace where all of you will be accepted."

Maggie's lips parted. Dylan had to swallow down the desire that rose. This was a business arrangement, just like the guys had outlined in the barn. He could do this.

"You'd do that?" she asked.

"Sure," said Dylan. "It's the only way I think this little guy will let me put him down."

Maggie grinned at Spin with so much love and

care in her eyes. She'd said she'd only had the dog for a few days. She'd rescued him, healed him, and given him a new lease on life. Dylan wondered if feelings that deep could develop so quickly and last longer than a dog's lifetime?

CHAPTER EIGHT

Maggie rolled over in her bed. Her legs tangled in the top sheet. She'd been dreaming of a strong, warm, male body with corded muscles, a serious facade, kind eyes and a scent that reminded her of a fall day.

She'd tossed and turned all night. Now that her eyes were open, everything was bleary. She couldn't help feeling that yesterday had been some sort of dream. But she knew it had been real.

She'd been proposed to.

Sort of.

Dylan had offered more of a business proposal than a potential love match.

The very idea was crazy. But the idea wouldn't leave her alone. It kept buzzing around her brain, sneaking into her dreams, and nagging her now that she was awake.

She flung her arms out across her bed and met fur. Sugar rested on the right side of the bed, snoring softly. Stevie sat awake at the foot of her bed, waiting patiently for her to rise. The two smaller dogs rested comfortably in their doggie beds on the floor. Spin sulked in the closet where Maggie saw his eyes flash at her.

Maggie was certain she knew what the dog was thinking. Why are we here alone in this drafty apartment when we could be on a ranch with space to roam and run free? We could be working alongside animals who were trained in the noble cause of helping wounded soldiers. And we could be spending time getting closer to one of said soldiers who'd offered his home, his support, and his hand in marriage.

Maggie flung herself back on the other side of the bed, turning away from Spin's accusing glare. When she did, Stevie woke up with a confused bark, which woke up the smaller dogs. By the time she sat up, her entire household was awake and looking to her for their sustenance, healing, and direction in life.

Her dogs had been immediately taken by Dylan.

Dogs were good judges of character, after all. It was clear that Dylan was doing an honorable thing in trying to save the ranch for the wounded soldiers in his care. And he had kind eyes. Beautiful eyes, set in a face so handsome that Maggie shuddered under the warm covers.

The idea was preposterous; marrying a stranger. Sure, she knew people did it all the time. Pastor Patel and his wife had been matched by their families. The two had married only after a few weeks of meeting for the first time. She knew that the Patels were very happy, with a large family of adult children—some of whom were matched in the same light.

The thought of that sounded nice; having parents who knew her so well that they succeeded in finding her the love of her life. Having parents she trusted enough to ask for their assistance in matters of the heart.

Maggie had never known that kind of parental inquisitiveness. Her parents had barely known her at all before they abandoned her. Her foster parents only cared that she did as she was told. They didn't take a singular interest in her outside of her duties as their free childcare and maid service.

Pastor Patel was the one person in the world who

knew her best. And he said that Dylan was a match for her. It bared a moment's thought. It had deserved that night of tossing and turning. Maybe even a full day of pondering.

Maggie threw off the covers, upsetting the lounging dogs all around her. She got up and went to the bathroom. She handled her morning business and then went to her closet. But the thoughts followed her around.

Dylan had made his offer so calmly, so logically so that it all made sense. Marry him, live and work on the ranch, and everyone gets what they want. And then there was Pastor Patel with his compatibility argument. But they both missed one thing; love.

Maggie wanted to be in love when she got married. If she ever got married. The way things had gone in her love life, she had already begun to doubt she ever would. So her lack of love life would be a better statement.

But if she said yes, she could have a love life. Not only that, she could have a home. She could have a man who would stand up for her, a built-in family with the other men of the ranch, and a place for her animals.

Why was she hesitating again? Oh, yeah. She didn't love him.

But she didn't doubt that she could if given the opportunity. The question was, would he give her the opportunity? Would he offer up his love in return?

But did she really need his love? She'd been in the system and enough foster homes to know that most people only wanted her because she could fill a need. There was a need for her at the ranch. Just like she had in the foster system, she could sit quietly and make herself useful so that Dylan and the other soldiers would keep her.

This would be no different. She didn't need love, just a place to belong for as long as she could.

A sound at the front door, had her tossing on her robe. It didn't sound like a knock, but there was definitely someone out there. The dogs trailed her out of the bedroom. Maggie looked through the peephole and only saw someone retreating. It was her landlord. She opened the door when the coast was clear. But the storm had landed on her door and left its destruction.

An eviction notice hung from her door knocker. Well, that was that. She really had no choice. But she did have options.

She pulled out a suitcase and began to pack. She'd take Dylan up on his offer of thirty days. She'd try and see if she could fit into his life. She'd make herself useful, make herself scarce, and maybe he'd let her stay forever.

CHAPTER NINE

Dylan tossed and turned in his bed. His leg tangled in the sheets. He'd been dreaming of soft curves, hair like falling, brown leaves in autumn, intelligent eyes that shied away from a direct gaze, and the subtle scent of roses mixed with a hint of something that reminded him of the bear-skinned rug in his father's hunting cabin.

He couldn't get the thought of Maggie Shaw out of his mind.

He'd asked her to marry him. He thought he'd never utter those words to another woman in his life. But the words had come unbidden from his lips, and he'd meant them.

Oh, he didn't imagine himself in love or anything foolish like that. To him, Maggie and her dogs were another set of beings he could rescue. There was a sadness, an apartness about her that was familiar to him. He knew, without a doubt, that the Purple Heart Ranch would heal her internal wounds just like they were healing his external ones.

That was the only reason he'd offered to help her. And if she said yes, he'd be certain to make that clear. Unlike what Dr. Patel thought, Dylan's heart was not a part of the equation.

Dylan pushed himself up to a sitting position. With the covers turned around his good leg, his stump was on clear display. He looked down at the hunk of meat that was all that was left of his leg. He'd been having a fevered dream about a brown-eyed girl, but looking down at his reality was better than a cold shower.

He went through his morning ritual of cleaning the stump. Infection was always a concern for an amputee. He rolled on the liner over his stump. His first prosthetic had been a newer model with a silicone liner, but it never felt quite right to him. A bad fitting prosthetic did more harm than good. So, Dylan kept it old school.

Over the liner, he slid a prosthetic sock to hold the limb in place. And finally, he slipped his stump into the prosthetic limb. Standing, he pressed his body weight down until he heard the telltale audible signal of the pin clicking and locking into place.

Over his leg, he pulled on long cargo pants that hid both his legs. Though his natural leg was whole, it had not escaped unscathed. He had many scars on his shins and thighs from the explosion that had hit his entire unit.

Dylan never showed his leg to anyone but his physical therapist, Mark. Not since his family and his ex-fiancée had seen his stump and turned their backs on him. He would never go through that again.

So, what made him think he was marriage material now? Maggie had left shortly after his botched business proposal. Women wanted love and romance, not facts and logic. He doubted he'd ever see her again.

So imagine his surprise when he walked out of his cottage to see her beat up truck pulling up to his drive.

"So," she said out of the window. "Would I get my own room?"

"Of course." Dylan kept his hands behind his back, certain that if they were loose he'd reach out to her and pull her into a hug of gratitude.

"The dogs sleep inside," she stated in a tone that was non-negotiable.

"Absolutely."

"You expect me to cook and clean up I suppose." The wince that appeared on her rounded face could only be described as adorable.

"I expect us both to cook and do household chores," he said. "You're not a domestic worker, Maggie. We'll be partners."

That got a surprise rise of her eyebrows. She was looking at Dylan head on. No more shy side gaze. In that unguarded moment, Dylan saw her clearly. And he liked what he saw.

"Thirty days?" she asked.

"Thirty days," he confirmed. "And then we decide."

Maggie bit her lip. Dylan had to look away. He was dying to know what her bottom lip tasted like. With this arrangement, it wasn't like he'd ever get a sample of that delicacy.

Maggie opened the door. Before she could step down, Dylan was at her side, offering his hand. She took it and climbed down.

He didn't immediately let go of her hand once she was securely on the ground. He wasn't sure why? The pads of her fingers were rough, not soft. She was a hard-worker. He knew that by her profession. He also knew that she'd seen death. Likely not of a human being, but watching helpless animals die had to take a toll.

Dylan rubbed his thumb over her finger pads. She looked at him uncertainly. The sound of barking broke their study of each other. One by one, they unloaded the animals. Spin bounced excitedly on his front paws when Dylan handed him down from his crate and Maggie attached his apparatus.

"Come on," he said. "Let me show you all around the ranch."

The dogs nipped at their heels as they began their tour. He'd had to let Maggie's hand go as they took the dogs down. Maggie led the partially blind Rottweiler around on a leash with one hand. She carried the Chihuahua with the missing paw around in her other arm.

He wasn't sure what to say to her. They kept looking over at each other and then immediately looking away. It was worse than the first day of middle school.

But the silence wasn't uncomfortable. And the dogs occupied most of their attention. The pack of animals was excited to be in new surroundings and sniffed at every leaf and bush they came into contact with.

"There you are, Dylan."

Dylan looked up to see his trainer, Mark. Mark was a good ten years older than Dylan, but the man didn't look it. He was tall and well built. When the few women that came by the ranch stopped by, their gazes always found and lingered on Mark.

Dylan turned to Maggie. Her gaze wasn't on Mark. It was on the horse he led.

Dylan couldn't blame Maggie for that. Bailey was a beautiful specimen of horseflesh. She was a gentle creature and well trained. So, she didn't spook when the small animals came near.

"Hey, Bailey," said Dylan as he reached out to the horse. "You're looking good today."

The horse bowed her head and gave a soft whinny.

"And who do we have here?" Mark prompted, eyes on Maggie.

"This is Maggie. She's ..." Dylan looked at Maggie. Should he call her his fiancée? She hadn't exactly accepted his proposal. They were just trying things out for a while. So what did that make her? She's my girlfriend."

Maggie's eyes did that wide thing again that

allowed Dylan to see into the depths of her being. It was surprise and something else. Dylan decided he liked it. He'd have to find other ways to get that rise out of her.

He realized he also liked that title on her. Girl-friend. Soon fiancée. Maybe one day, wife.

CHAPTER TEN

Maggie shook the hand of the trainer—what was his name again? Oh, yeah; Martin? No, Mark. Something that began with M. She had no idea. No other words registered after Dylan said that single word.

Girlfriend.

Dylan had called her his girlfriend. She'd never been anyone's girlfriend before. She'd only been on a handful of dates in her entire life. But now she was someone's girlfriend.

Logically, she understood why he'd decided on that title. She'd seen the decision making in his blue eyes. He couldn't call her his fiancée. She hadn't entirely agreed to that.

But they were dating in a sense. They were

taking time to get to know each other. Time to see if they would suit as a couple. That qualified her as his girlfriend.

Maggie's chest puffed up at the new title she now carried. Her head swam high enough to reach a cloud with this new role. She had a boyfriend. And one that was not too shabby if she did say so herself.

Dylan hadn't balked when she insisted her dogs stay inside. He'd even divvied up the domestic chores. What man does that?

What man, indeed? Maybe he was gay? Maybe he was using her as his beard to hide that fact.

But no. Pastor Patel was his psychologist, surely he'd know if Dylan wasn't truly interested in Maggie. There was also the way he'd looked at her when she'd pulled up in his drive that morning.

There had been relief in his raised brow. But there had been something else at the corner of his eyes. Just a flash, but she'd seen it. It looked to her like interest. It was possible that he had more than a business interest in her.

Maggie was definitely interested. Dylan was handsome, thoughtful, and kind. Where was a pen? She was ready to sign on the dotted line to make this man hers for a lifetime.

But right now she was his girlfriend. She let the

word wash over her again. She remembered the feel of his fingers rubbing her thumb as though he could take off the rough calluses and smooth things over. She had a feeling he could.

Those fingers now rubbed Spin's head. The mutt looked at her smugly. That was fine. Spin might be in the running for this particular man's best friend. But Maggie was currently his girlfriend.

A girlfriend got handholding. She got long walks. She got taken to dinner.

Hmmm? These were all benefits a pet enjoyed from their humans. But, so what. Maggie would take it.

Maggie chanced a glance up at her new boyfriend. He worried his lip, as though he were insecure about the title he'd just given her. Maggie smiled brightly at him, trying to communicate her acceptance of the role. Then she decided to use her words.

"Hi." She stuck out her hand to the trainer. Mark —that was his name. "I'm Maggie, Dylan's girlfriend."

"So I've heard." Mark smiled and gave Maggie's hand a polite shake.

As Mark released her hand the horse scooted over to the fence and rubbed itself against the wooden planks. Maggie's eyes zeroed in on the horse's rear. She noted that there was a patch of inflamed skin there.

"Is she suffering from Sweet Itch?" Maggie asked.

"Yeah," said Mark. "I just sprayed her down with repellent but those midges seem to like the way she tastes."

"Have you put a fan in her stables in the evening? Midges and gnats like to come out in the evening and find damp places or areas where there's stagnant water."

"You know," Mark scratched at his chin, "that's a good idea. I didn't know you were dating a vet, Banks."

Maggie opened her mouth to correct the trainer, but Dylan beat her to it.

"She's a vet tech," he said. "She's very dedicated to animals."

Dylan smiled down at her. His brow raised again, lifting with what looked like relief, stretching wide with what looked like interest. Maggie needed a fan under his gaze. She felt suddenly hot and damp all over.

"She's going to help out around here," Dylan continued.

"There are also some foods I can recommend,"

Maggie said. "Sweet Itch is often a sign of a compromised immune system. I could write up a list."

"Why don't we chat about it on the way to the stables?" said Mark. "It's time for Dylan's training session."

"That would be great," Maggie beamed.

"No."

Both Maggie and Mark turned to stare at Dylan. His single word had been forcefully said. His eyes, wide and open only a moment ago, were now narrowed and hooded.

Dylan cleared his throat, but the tension was still there in his clenched jaw. "I mean, you should go and get settled in, Maggie."

He didn't look directly at her. Instead, his gaze was on her ear. Maggie resisted the urge to tug at her ear. Just as she knew what interest looked like, she was more familiar with what disinterest looked like. Dylan was not interested in her coming along to his training sessions.

As further proof of her assumption, he handed Spin to her. When his forearms and hands brushed hers, there was no spark. Instead, a shiver went through her body.

Dylan's gaze flicked to hers for just a brief

second, and then he looked away again. "I'll see you when I get home this evening."

And with that, he turned to Mark and walked away. Mark gave her an apologetic shrug, then he and the horse turned to follow Dylan.

Dylan walked away stiffly. He took with him all the closeness they'd built. Once again Maggie was left standing alone and shut out.

CHAPTER ELEVEN

Dylan was sore after his session, but not just physically. Something ached inside him. Something he couldn't yet work out. The whole ride he couldn't get the look on Maggie's face out of his mind.

They had had a great time in the span of walking from his house to the training grounds. When he'd called her his girlfriend, he'd initially tripped over the word. But it hadn't felt like a lie. It felt like a newly discovered truth.

Until he'd went and ruined it.

But he couldn't let her see him train. His leg was awkward and stiff as he mounted the horse. He couldn't cast it over the horse's back. He needed a hand. He used his own hand, refusing to allow Mark or the others to assist him.

Beyond that, his sessions were often brutal, mainly because he pushed himself. Dylan was a true believer in the adage No Pain, No Gain. If it didn't hurt him a little, he was certain he wasn't working hard enough.

He wouldn't have minded her watching him ride. Even when he pushed himself, he felt powerful in the mount, riding high on the horse. But then there was the dismounting, which was even trickier than the mounting after he'd pushed his muscles so hard.

No. He didn't want Maggie to see that; weak and vulnerable. The last time he'd allowed anyone to see his weakness it had crushed his spirit.

Dylan had liked the way Maggie had looked at him today. She'd looked up to him like he was capable, like he was her savior. Better that she look disappointed for a short time, rather than look down with pity on him for the rest of their lives.

He had to remind himself, and her, that this wouldn't be some great love affair. This was a practical arrangement. They could be friendly. They might even become friends. But love wasn't in the cards for someone like him. Someone who didn't have their whole selves to offer.

He knew a woman like Maggie deserved more. But as much as he was doing this for the soldiers in need of this ranch, he was also doing it for himself. It felt good to have a woman near. To have a woman on his arm. To have a woman gaze upon him like he was a full and complete man.

So, even though he was more sore than he'd been in months after a training session, Dylan set a quick pace back to his house. When he came upon the small cottage, the lights were on in the kitchen. He saw movement through the window. He heard the excited barking of dogs, more like begging whimpers.

Dylan opened the back door to the smell of ... something burning.

His training immediately set in. He took a quick glance around the room to assess the danger. There was one pan on fire. A pot of boiling water spilled over onto the stovetop. And smoke plumed out of the oven.

Maggie looked up at him. Her hair was frazzled. There was a smear of something—grease? food?—on her cheek. A mix of panic, defeat, and shame dimmed her usually expressive eyes. "I'm sorry."

Dylan rushed into action, stepping over and around barking, yipping dogs as he did so. He put the burning pan into the sink. He shut off all the burners. Then he opened the oven door to allow the smoke to make a full escape.

"I'm sorry," Maggie repeated again. "I was trying to make grown-up food."

Dylan pulled out a charred steak from the oven. The dogs all took steps back and moaned at the travesty. Dylan recognized potatoes in the pot of water, but they knocked audibly against the bottom of the pan as though the boiling water hadn't affected the spuds at all. He wasn't sure what had been in the pan? Maybe greens? But they were now brown.

"I've only ever cooked for kids and animals," Maggie said. "I'm great with hot dogs and chicken nuggets and fries."

"I like hot dogs, nuggets, and fries." He offered her a smile, but she was too busy scrubbing at the mess on his stove to notice.

"Really?" she asked as she mopped up the spilled water. "I took you for a fine dining kind of guy."

"What gave you that impression?" Dylan pulled out the frozen fare from the freezer.

"Pictures of your family." She turned and faced him, eyes wide with guilt. "I wasn't snooping. They were on the mantel. You were all at some fancy place."

Dylan nodded. "My father won't eat out unless a place has a Michelin star, and my mother won't eat food portions bigger than her thumb."

"But not you?"

"Not me."

Maggie chuckled at his words, the tension visibly seeping from her shoulders.

Dylan's palms felt warm even though he held frozen foods in his hands. He pulled out a pan from the cupboard, sprayed, and laid out the food. "What about you?"

"Me?" The tension crept back into her shoulders, and she looked away from him. She sat down in one of the chairs and lifted Soldier into her arms. The Chihuahua licked at whatever was on her chin. Dylan felt a hint of jealousy towards the little dog.

"I don't have family," Maggie said. "My parents abandoned me at a young age. I was in an orphanage until I was a teenager. I assumed I'd be there until I turned eighteen. I got fostered. But that family just wanted me as an unpaid nanny to their younger kids."

She said all of this while caressing and cuddling Soldier in one hand. With the other, she reached down and scratched Stevie behind the ear. Dylan had the strongest urge to take her into his arms and hug her. Instead, he poured her a glass of juice and placed it in front of her.

Maggie accepted his offering. She was starting to make sense to him. A woman who'd been abandoned as a child, who'd dedicated her life to saving wounded animals. A woman who hadn't known parental love now trying to find a way to fit in and make herself useful.

Maggie had been discarded and misused, just like her animals. Dylan needed to let her know that he wouldn't do that to her. He wanted to tell her that she had a place here for as long as she wanted. He wanted to guarantee her forever.

A place. Not his heart. He could guarantee her a place forever so that she finally felt at home.

"Maggie," he said softly, then waited until she lifted her gaze to him. "I know our relationship is essentially a business relationship. But I was thinking, maybe we could be friends? What do you say we get to know each other?"

CHAPTER TWELVE

Her new boyfriend, and possible fiancé, and potential husband wanted to be her friend. Was this ranch some kind of alternate universe where plain girls got the prince?

And he could cook.

Maggie opened the door to the oven and took the fries out. This time there was no smoke accompanying the meal. The spuds were golden brown and cooked through.

When Dylan had appeared at the door, she'd expected him to blow a fuse at the sight of his once pristine kitchen. She'd noticed that about him. Not that he was prone to anger. That he was very ... orderly was putting it nicely.

The furniture was high quality. The knickknacks

dispersed around the small home would be better labeled as accouterments.

Dylan had said he wasn't into fine dining. He may not hunger for expensive things, but he certainly had expensive tastes.

Maggie still wore many of the hand-me-downs and Goodwill items from her senior year in high school. What few furnishings she had were all second-hand. She wasn't certain that she could measure up to this guy.

"Ketchup or mustard?" he asked, holding up both condiments.

"Both."

"Me too," he grinned. "Relish?"

Maggie wrinkled her nose at the offensive suggestion. "Pickles belong on burgers. Or in tartar sauce for fish nuggets."

"So it shall be decreed," Dylan said with a grin. He put the relish back in the fridge.

Turning toward the plates of bunned hot dogs, Dylan maneuvered around the excited dogs nipping at his feet. Maggie noticed he stepped carefully over and around them, but he did so stiffly. He hadn't told her what his injury was from the war, but she'd had an inkling since the first day they'd met. Though he made a concerted effort to maintain an even gait, Dylan favored his left leg.

Having dressed the hot dogs, he reached into the cupboard where she'd placed the dog food. His pant leg hitched, and she saw the barest glint of metal instead of a fleshy ankle.

Self-consciously, he reached back and yanked his pant leg down. Quickly, Maggie averted her gaze. It hadn't taken her long to realize the reason for his curt dismissal of her at the training fields had been because he didn't want her to see him struggle with his injury.

Dylan turned, but by then Maggie was already looking down. She placed the fries on the plate next to the wieners. Still, she caught him giving his right pant leg another tug to hide his wound before bending down on his good knee.

He poured out a measured cup and placed it in the bowls, giving each dog a scratch behind the ear or pat on the back.

He straightened a bit awkwardly, using the counter to help him back to his feet. Maggie continued arranging the fries until he'd resumed his full height.

She understood wounded animals and their need to hide their injuries. She'd have to back off until he came to her and saw that she meant him no harm, she was no threat. She wanted to care for him. She'd simply have to wait him out until he trusted her and allowed it.

Feeding a wounded animal was usually a good ploy. But she'd failed spectacularly at that. Now that she had his help in the kitchen, things were smoothing out a bit.

Dylan washed his hands and then they sat at the table with their food. He reached out his hand to hers. Maggie stared at his open palm.

"I bless my food before eating it," he said.

"Me too. I just—I mean—" She shut up and handed him her hands. There was that spark of awareness again. She lifted her gaze to his and knew, the rise of his brow and the flare of his nostril, that he'd felt it too.

Dylan said a blessing over the food. Then he released his hold on her, but Maggie still felt a connection between them.

They took a few bites in silence appreciating the simple fare. A smidge of ketchup dotted his jaw and she giggled. He grinned, wiped at the smudge. Then he pointed his red fingertip at her.

Maggie wiped at her cheek. She felt a dollop of moisture there. When she pulled her thumb away, she came away with a glob of mustard. She grinned, popping her thumb into her mouth and getting rid of the evidence.

When her gaze lifted to Dylan's, his smile had slipped, his gaze still locked on hers. There was heat in his blue eyes. It made her shiver.

Dylan sat his half-eaten hot dog down and rose. He went to the freezer and grabbed a few ice cubes. They plopped with a splash into his glass of water before he sat down again.

"So, Dylan." Maggie struggled for a topic of conversation that didn't have to do with animals or her lack of kitchen skills. "What branch of the military were you in?"

"Army. I was a Sergeant E-5."

"I don't know what that means? I don't know much about the military and rank."

"It's a fancy sounding title that let me boss other men around."

He was grinning again. Maggie felt she was on safe ground with him once more. "Where were you ... stationed in the war?"

"I was deployed," he corrected her. "We're not technically at war. I spent three years in the armed forces. Mostly as a part of Operation Inherent Resolve in Syria and then in Operation Resolute

Support in Afghanistan."

"It's most dangerous in Afghanistan, isn't it?"

Dylan shrugged. "There are operations stationed all around the world in areas where civilians vacation."

"Do you not want to talk about it?"

Dylan flexed his arms behind his head and leaned back. Maggie tried not to stare, but even his biceps were attractive. She wondered what it would be like to be inside his embrace.

"You'll find that most soldiers don't want to talk about it." His words were blunt, but he couched them with a small smile. "It's hard to talk about it with someone who wasn't there."

"Okay." Maggie finished off her hot dog and wiped her mouth. She looked down at the full-bellied dogs who were all laid out on the floor at their feet.

Dylan chewed at his lower lip. He rubbed his forefinger around the lip of the glass. All the while, Maggie held her breath and hoped.

"I lost my leg in the last mission I was on." He said it so quietly she thought she'd imagined it. "We were helping the local forces to build a school in Afghanistan. The locals were thankful. They were so full of hope."

He took a deep breath. Maggie thought he might not continue. But she knew there was nothing for her to do but stay quiet and still and let him come to her.

"We were all so full of hope. We were all a part of that mission. The entire squad didn't make it. Those of us that did ... we all lost something that day. That's why we're here. We're trying to rebuild ... our lives."

Spin made his way over to Dylan. He gave a whimper, and Dylan picked up the dog. Placing the terrier in his lap, Dylan stroked behind his ears.

"You made this apparatus yourself?" asked Dylan.

"I tinkered with the design. An original could cost a couple hundred bucks. Most families looking to adopt a dog aren't willing to fork out the expense or the time. That's why wounded animals get put down so often."

Dylan gazed at her as he continued to stroke Spin's coat. "The Purple Heart Ranch is dedicated to rehabilitating the wounded."

"I know. I'd like to help." Before she could think better of it she added, "The animals as well as the soldiers."

Dylan's throat worked before he answered. "It's different with humans, Maggie. Men especially.

Nothing on this earth has more pride than a wounded man."

"I don't agree. I've found healing has one constant ingredient; patience."

He didn't argue. He didn't meet her gaze again. "It's been a long day. We're all tired. I'll walk you to your room."

Dylan sat Spin back on the floor as he stood. Together, and in silence, they cleared their plates and loaded them into the dishwasher. With the kitchen clean, Dylan reached out his hand to her. She didn't hesitate. She took hold of his hand and walked with him down the hall. The dogs trailed in their wake.

It was a short walk to the door of her bedroom. Once outside the door, he paused. She turned to him. There were only a few inches between them. He'd loosened his hold on her hand, but he still held onto a few of her fingertips. Slowly, his gaze lifted to hers.

Maggie's heart raced. Was he going to kiss her? They'd just had dinner and conversation. Before that, it had been a stroll around a ranch. This was practically a second date, at least by her measure.

She watched him gulp, watched his chest work.

Slowly, he pulled his fingers away from hers, one by one.

"I'm really glad you're here," he said. "I think we can make this work. I can't give you everything a true husband can. But if you agree to be my wife, we can save this place, and I can offer you this home, and a sense of security, and my protection."

As proposals went, that was practically perfect.

"I'm not rushing you," he continued. "We have time. I just want you to know that you would always have a place. Even if we lose the ranch. You and your dogs would have a place to stay with me."

Maggie's heart was doing flips. She was certain he could hear it.

"Anyway," he took a step back. "Good night, Maggie."

He took another step back and bumped into Spin. Maggie clenched her hands into fists and glued them to her sides so she wouldn't reach out to help Dylan as he wobbled. She knew it would not be appreciated, though she ached to do it.

Dylan righted himself, then he reached down to pet Spin. The dog looked up at him with pure adoration. Maggie knew her eyes were doing the same. To hide her burgeoning feelings, she turned and opened her bedroom door. Four dogs rushed in to claim their spots. One remained on the other side of the threshold.

Spin looked between Maggie and Dylan. Then he wheeled himself closer to Dylan.

"It's fine," Dylan said scooping up the dog. "He can hang with me tonight."

The two of them disappeared into the room at the end of the hall. Maggie shut the other dogs and herself inside her room. It was going to take a lot of patience, but she was determined to get closer to her wounded soldier.

CHAPTER THIRTEEN

There was a warm body lying next to Dylan in his bed. He reached for it instinctively bringing it inside his embrace like he'd wanted to do all through dinner. Like he'd wanted to do when he'd walked her to her bedroom door. He'd entwined his fingers with hers without thinking about what he was doing. That was how strong his attraction was to Maggie. He sought her out whenever she was near, like a magnet finding its charge. But when he reached out this time, seeking her positivity, instead of warm, womanly curves he felt fur.

Dylan opened his eyes just in time to see a wet tongue lap him up from his chin to his cheek. The smell of doggie breath had him turning away. But

Spin simply pawed at Dylan until he had his attention again.

The dog's tail wagged and thumped his front paws so animatedly that Dylan couldn't be upset. He gave the dog a scratch, trying not to think about the woman who had rescued him. The woman who was making Dylan feel things he hadn't in a long time, things he never thought he'd feel again.

Dylan lifted himself and swung his leg over the bed. Spin pulled himself over to the edge of the bed and looked down at the floor. Dylan bent over and brought the dog's apparatus up on the bed. He'd taken both his apparatus and the dog's off last night before they both curled up on the mattress and fell into a deep sleep. Now he hooked the dog into the contraption and set Spin on the floor. Then Dylan turned to his own leg.

Spin eyed the rump that was left of Dylan's leg. He ventured closer and sniffed it. Spin gave a nod of his head, as though he accepted Dylan's state. Then he took off to explore the rest of Dylan's room, wheeling around his bed and into his closet.

Dylan smiled after the dog. The dog's easy acceptance thawed something in Dylan's heart. If only every living soul could be so accepting of his wound. A knock at the bedroom door sent Dylan reaching for the covers to hide his mangled leg.

"Dylan?" called Maggie from the other side of the door. "Are you up?"

Panic settled over Dylan. It would take him a few moments to get his prosthetic on, but not before cleaning the area first. And then he'd have to get to his closet to find a long pair of pants to cover the apparatus.

"Don't come in," he shouted.

"I won't."

There had been the sound of morning sun in her voice when she'd knocked on his door. Dylan clearly heard a cloud in her tone now. He hung his head in his hands. Just last night he'd promised to be her protector. And yet at every turn, he kept hurting her.

"I wouldn't do that," she said from the other side of the door, her voice still small but filled with a compassion that brushed the rough edges of his heart. "I told Mark I'd help him this morning with the Sweet Itch problem. I just wanted to let you know where I was going."

Dylan removed the blanket from his leg and rubbed at the ache there. It wasn't soothed. The pain was lower, in his shin—a shin that was no longer there. He was a constant sufferer of phantom pains, but more so these past couple of days.

He watched Spin go to the door. The terrier wagged his tail at the sound of his owner's voice. A part of Dylan wanted to do the same. He wanted to open up to Maggie, but he couldn't even open the door. He didn't want her to see him like this.

"I'm putting the dogs in the backyard so they'll stay out of trouble," she continued through the wooden barrier. "You can put Spin there, too. Or take him with you. It's up to you."

Dylan looked down at the dog. The dog looked between Dylan and the door as though he didn't understand why there was a barrier between the three of them. The phantom cramp returned to Dylan's absent leg. No matter how much he massaged it, it never left him. It was always there.

"Do you need anything ... from me?" she asked.

There was so much he wanted from her. But he could never ask it. "Thanks, Maggie. I'll catch up with you later, okay?"

"Sure ... sure."

He waited until he heard the sound of her steps, followed by many feet padding across the wood floor. He waited until he heard the heavy back door shut. Only then did he go through the motions of putting himself together.

Maggie had tried to sound positive, but he'd heard it. He'd turned her brightness to something dim. Maybe this was a mistake. He kept taking two steps forward with her, only to remember he couldn't stand on his own two feet and fall back.

Dylan showered, taking special care to clean his stump. When he was finished, he dried himself, taking special care around his missing limb before he put on the prosthetic.

After getting dressed, he led Spin to the back door. The dog took one look outside, then looked back up at him. Seemed the dog had no intentions of leaving Dylan's side, but he'd have to. Dylan wouldn't be able to keep an eye on the dog and do his chores.

With a firm command, he urged the dog out the door. Spin made a grumbling sound, and he did as he was told, but not before casting one more forlorn look over his shoulder. Dylan almost laughed, but he was feeling too low to muster up the sound.

"How's wedded bliss?" asked Fran when he met Dylan on the path to the training fields.

Dylan grimaced, his facial features scrunching

up into confused angles. When he let his face relax, he sighed.

"That bad?"

"She's amazing. I just ... It's only ..." Dylan sighed again.

"Because if you don't want to marry her, I'm sure X would have no problem manning up." Fran pointed off in the distance.

Dylan had to shade his eyes, but then he saw it. Xavier was leaning against the fencing. He had his cowboy hat pulled low. He leaned in and said something to Maggie. She startled. And then she laughed, brushing her hair over her shoulders. Dylan knew that when a woman brushed her hair away it was a sign that she was interested.

His feet were in motion before he realized. His prosthetic struck the ground with purpose as he moved toward the two.

Maggie looked up as though sensing his presence. She'd been smiling at Xavier, but when she spied Dylan her face lit up like it was the sun dawning.

Dylan nearly tripped at the brightness of her smile. He reached out to the railing to steady himself. She was within his reach. He felt the pull to her again. It was too strong to resist.

And so he reached out to her. At the first contact of his fingertips on her forearm, he felt a humming sensation tremble through his finger pads. That's what made his hand close her in a grasp and tug her into his side.

Maggie gasped, her eyes going wide in the open vulnerable way that did something to his insides. Dylan circled his arm around her back. When he did, his palm crossed over capable shoulders able to handle a heavy load. His instinct was to take all the weight away and heft it onto his own back.

Maggie came willingly into his embrace, fitting perfectly into the space between his arm and chest. Warmth spread through Dylan. But that's not what made him know he was in trouble.

When he looked up, he saw both Xavier and Fran smirking at him.

CHAPTER FOURTEEN

Maggie hated simpering women. Women who shrank like violets and didn't speak when men came around. Women who let men speak for them and no longer said anything intelligent when their significant other came into the room.

She was standing in the open air. She'd been having an interesting conversation with a man. A very handsome man at that. Xavier Ramos could only be called beautiful.

He'd been flirting with her, in that way where men didn't really mean it. Where their entire vocabulary consisted of come-ons because they didn't know how to engage a woman's brain. Xavier's interest in her wasn't true. He was flirting because it was in his nature.

Maggie hadn't been bothered by it. They both knew he wasn't serious. It felt more like he was feeling her out than actually checking her out.

Maggie appreciated that. It meant he was looking out for Dylan. This was a preformed squad she was walking into. A cohesive unit. A battle-hardened, well-suited family. And it seemed like she was being accepted. First by Fran, who'd greeted her and walked her to the stables to find Mark. Then by Mark, who'd listened to her suggestions and ideas to heal the ailing horses.

She was sure she'd won over Xavier by not taking his bait. She was certain they all saw her as an intelligent, capable woman.

Then the moment Dylan showed up, the words slowly seeped out of her brain. When his arm made its way around her shoulder, she forgot how to breathe. She didn't shrink into herself out of shyness. She didn't recoil from his touch. She melted into his welcome heat with an aim to become a part of him.

"Don't you have somewhere to be, X?" Dylan growled. But Maggie didn't mind. The reverb sent a tingle down to her toes.

"Just making nice with the prettiest lady on the ranch." Xavier winked at her.

That snapped Maggie out of it. She laughed at Xavier's fake flirting. "I'm pretty sure I'm the only woman on the ranch, outside of the four-legged variety."

"Well, your legs are—"

"That's enough." Dylan cut Xavier off with another low growl.

Dylan's voice made Maggie jump, but Xavier only smirked. He tilted his hat to Maggie. Then he smirked again at Dylan before taking off.

Fran gave her a friendly smile and then gave Dylan the same smirk.

Maggie turned to face Dylan but found that she couldn't. His grip on her shoulder was vise-like.

Was he jealous?

That was absurd. No one had ever had any cause to get jealous over her. But Dylan's grip was really tight, as though she were something he had no plans to let go of or share.

"Dylan? Are you ... I mean ... This might sound silly but ..."

His grip loosened now that his friends had disappeared into the stables. Maggie turned to face him, feeling less brave now that she was looking up into his blue eyes. He looked uncomfortable and shifted his weight from one leg to the other.

"Ramos is a good guy," said Dylan. "I trust him with my life. But he's bad news with women."

"Why is that information necessary for me to know?"

Dylan looked even more uncomfortable.

He *was* jealous. She might not know men well. But she knew animal behavior. He was exhibiting the telltale markers of having his territory threatened. She was his territory. She didn't mind him prowling around her perimeter. But she needed him to know that she had no plans to stay.

"I gave you my word," Maggie said. "I'm not the kind of girl to play around on a guy. I wouldn't know how. I've never had a boyfriend."

Dylan eased up his hold. Maggie regretted the loosening embrace, but she wanted any show of affection to be genuine and not some alpha male reaction.

"I didn't take Xavier seriously. He was kinda funny. Not as funny as he thinks though."

Dylan looked slightly less uncomfortable. He chewed at his lower lip as he'd done last night at dinner. It was like he was chewing over the words he wanted to say, seeing if they were bitter or sweet before he offered them up.

"I was wondering if you'd like to have lunch with me? In the Big House this time. We have a cook."

"Oh." Maggie felt her grin spread stupidly-wide. "I'd like that."

Dylan nodded, meeting her gaze now. Neither of them moved. A gentle breeze ruffled the ends of their hair. The sound of a bird's cry and the answering call filled the air.

"Sergeant Banks, there you are."

The spell broke. Maggie and Dylan turned to face a man in a suit. The man reminded Maggie of Dr. Cooper. She did shrink away now, moving slightly behind Dylan. The Cooper doppelgänger looked entirely out of place on the ranch.

"I'm glad I caught you in person," said the man. "I wanted to deliver this notice to you."

Dylan took the proffered papers. Maggie's heart sank with recognition as she spied the bold letters on the document. For the second time this week, she saw the word EVICTION in bright, red letters.

"You said we had until the end of the month to file," said Dylan.

"I'm sorry." The man didn't sound sorry in the least. "They want their hands on this land. If there was something I could do, I would. This goes through at the end of the week. Unless you're getting married in a couple of days, I don't see how this could be turned around."

"We are getting married tomorrow."

Both men looked over. Maggie nearly turned around herself. But she knew the sound of her own voice. She had said those words. She had made that proclamation.

"Who are you?" asked the man.

"I'm his fiancée." Maggie reached down and entwined her fingers with Dylan's. "And like I said, we're getting married tomorrow."

She looked to Dylan for confirmation. His gaze had widened as if to ask if she was sure. Maggie knew it could be thirty days, it could be three days. Her mind wouldn't change. She wanted to be with Dylan for the rest of her life.

As though he could read her mind, Dylan squeezed her fingers. The paper crumpled from his hand.

CHAPTER FIFTEEN

Dylan straightened his tie. The knot was perfect. The ends hung even.

The color brought out his eyes. He knew this because his mother had told him so when she'd bought it for him before he'd left for the army. She was always conscious of details regarding his outer appearance. But she had never once looked into his eyes and saw anything but the hue.

He yanked the knot and began the process over again.

He gave a gruff response to the knock at the door. Reed poked his head in the door. His grin preceding him as his prosthetic arm spread the door wide. Behind Reed, Sean slid into the door. He was sure to present the right side of his face, hiding the scars on the left.

"Man, you really cheated us not having a bachelor's party," said Reed. "We could've made a quick trip to Vegas."

Reed crossed his prosthetic arm over his chest. Unlike Dylan, he was not one to shy away from showing it.

Sean gave Dylan a full smile. With the injury on his face creasing into deep grooves, the smile spread deep into his skin.

"Being the good friends we are," Reed continued, " we do come bearing gifts."

"We'll take over your chores for the next couple of days," said Sean. "So you can enjoy your wedding night."

Both men waggled their eyebrows and made juvenile lewd gestures unbecoming of men their age and rank. Or so Dylan thought. The good humor fell from Dylan's face.

"It's not that type of marriage," he said.

The eyebrow waggling ceased. Both of the men's mouths dropped open in confusion. Their loss reminded Dylan of Sugar, Maggie's diabetic dog that didn't understand why he was constantly denied treats.

Sean and Reed looked at one another, then back at Dylan.

"It's a marriage of convenience," said Dylan.

"Maggie looks really convenient to me," said Reed.

Dylan narrowed his gaze at the man.

In response, Reed held up a plastic hand, metal glinting from his forearm. "For someone that's looking for convenience, you sure have a lot of feelings when it comes to this girl."

"I hardly know her." Dylan turned back to his tie, doing a quick and efficient knot and leaving it at that.

Sean turned to Reed and addressed the other man as though Dylan wasn't in the room. "Ramos told me he nearly bit his head off yesterday when he caught her talking to him," said Sean.

"Yeah, and I've seen the way he carries around her dog like it's their kid," said Reed.

Dylan knew if he denied it any further, the men would just keep ribbing him. So instead, he pulled on his jacket and headed for the door. The sounds of snickers followed him out of the room.

The ceremony was to be held in a gazebo near the pond. The three of them rode in a golf cart across the ranch to reach the area. Fran and Xavier had already set up chairs and a few Christmas deco-rations. It wouldn't be the wedding of the season that his mother and ex would've planned for him, but they had done their best. Dylan was touched. He just hoped Maggie wouldn't be too disappointed.

There was already a small gathering. Dr. Patel stood inside the gazebo. As an ordained minister, he had the power to officiate, which was good since the wedding was on such quick notice. But the man had been the one to suggest the match. For the past year, Dylan had put his mental health in the doctor's hands, and he hadn't disappointed him. Now he'd put his future, and maybe even his heart in Dr. Patel's hands.

He'd committed to seeing this through. He wanted to take care of Maggie. He wanted to be the one person she could always depend on. He wanted to be the cause of her comfort and her smiles and her eyes widening in joyous surprise. He wanted to take a closer look into her gaze and see what was past her brown eyes.

Dylan gave his head a shake. He had to remind himself; this wasn't some great romance. It was an arrangement, a convenience to them both.

They could be friends. It was fine for friends to look into one another's eyes to check on their health and well-being. That settled, Dylan walked down the aisle.

He saw the faces of his men, his friends. He saw the faces of his trainers and the ranch staff. No one looked doubtful about what he was doing. They all knew why this marriage was happening. It was saving their jobs, their livelihoods. But still, they were all smiling as Dylan took his place.

They'd all only known Maggie for a couple of days. But it seemed she had made quite an impression on everyone. Maggie's five dogs sat obediently at the front of the archway. Spin had been looking beyond the gazebo at the pond water, but he got up and wheeled his way to Dylan when he sensed the man's presence. Dylan bent down to give the dog a pat before he took his place before Dr. Patel.

The older man gave him a knowing smile. "How are you feeling?"

"This is the logical thing to do. I think we've both thought it through, and I'll take care of her."

A chuckle tickled out of Dr. Patel's mouth. Before the man could say more, his gaze lifted and his eyes lit.

Dylan turned to the way he'd just come and ceased being able to form a coherent thought.

Maggie stepped out of a golf cart with the help of

Fran. She wore a simple white dress. No frills, no embellishments. Just like her.

Dylan's palms felt moist, so he rubbed them against his pants. His neck felt hot, so he reached to loosen his tie. A thumping sound filled his ears, and he wondered if the horses had gotten loose. But no. It was his own heartbeat pounding.

Maggie looked nervous. She fidgeted. Dylan fought the need to go to her. He wanted to soothe her. He wanted to assure her that he would take care of her, that he would take care of it all. He wanted her to trust him, to believe in him.

Her gaze locked on him. She let out a breath that he would've sworn he felt tickle his nose. And then she began to move.

Faintly, Dylan heard music playing. But his gaze stayed trained on Maggie. With steady, sure steps, she came toward him. There was no sway in her hips. Just even strides toward him. Before he knew it, she stood before him.

Dylan heard Dr. Patel saying words. Lots of words in his calm, even tone. But Dylan paid the man no heed.

Instead, he watched Maggie's lips move. Her words made no sense to his head, but his heart pounded at the utterance.

He felt someone nudge him at his side. Dylan turned to glare at Fran who stood up beside him as his Best Man. Fran cocked his head toward Dr. Patel. The good doctor smiled at him and then repeated the words.

Dylan turned back to Maggie and said his vows. As each promise left his lips he was not surprised to realize that he meant every word. He intended to keep each vow; the vow he would make to Maggie, his bride.

"I pronounce you man and wife."

It was done. He was married. Maggie was his wife now, his responsibility. He wouldn't let her down. He wouldn't let any of them down.

"You may now kiss the bride."

Dylan stiffened. How had he forgotten that part? Maggie looked up at him with those wide eyes. Suddenly, the only thing in the world that he wanted to do was kiss this woman, his woman, his wife.

Dylan bent his head slowly, giving her every chance to back away. She didn't.

His lips met hers on the softest of brushes. She inhaled sharply but did not pull away. And so he pressed forward.

Maggie was everything soft and sweet. She was

willing and pliant. She was innocence and eagerness.

Dylan found his hand coming to the small of her back. She exhaled, and he drank in her essence, wanting more, needing more, taking more. He gave her torso a tug, and she came to him, fitting snuggly against his chest as he continued to press into her. She clicked into place.

There were cheers coming from a distance. And then he remembered where he was, where they were. He broke the kiss abruptly.

"I'm sorry," he said.

What had come over him?

Maggie's wide eyes narrowed, coming slowly back into focus. She averted her gaze and said nothing. So much for taking care of her. His first act of holy matrimony was to paw at his wife.

CHAPTER SIXTEEN

Maggie had to concentrate hard not to press her fingertips to her lips. They still tingled, even an hour after Dylan had kissed her. Her first kiss.

It had been everything she'd dreamed and more. With a man who she never could have imagined would be hers. And he was hers now.

She was Mrs. Dylan Banks.

The problem was that being Mrs. Dylan Banks felt very much like being Ms. Maggie Shaw. She and Dylan sat at their reception, which was dinner laid out in the ranch's equivalent of a mess hall. There was a store bought cake beside a heap of barbecue fare and grilled meat. The soldiers were having a grand time, laughing and clapping each other on the back, as well as clapping Dylan on the back.

Just about every one of the guys had come up to her and congratulated her and shared some funny story about Dylan. Even Sean, the most secluded soldier came over. Sean only gave her his good side when he spoke to her, but it was something. The only person that hadn't come up to her was her new husband.

Dylan stood at the grill turning hamburger patties until Reed shooed him away. Then he checked for more plates until Fran showed up with a stack. Dylan was the first to rise when someone asked for something else, anything else. And each time, everyone would shoo him down or away from the chore.

Finally, Maggie decided that she needed something that only her new husband could give her. She got up and went over to Dylan. When he saw her coming she detected a sense of wariness in his eyes.

Her steps faltered. He rose and took the last few toward her. He reached out his hand as though to bring her close. At the last second, he snatched it back.

"Did you need something?" Dylan asked. His voice wasn't gruff, but there was a note of hesitancy.

Was he regretting this? Their marriage? It hadn't even been twenty-four hours. She'd been passed over so many times in her life. Left abandoned and disappointed. He'd promised her that was over. Now it was time for him to make good on that promise.

"I was hoping we could have our first dance as husband and wife?" she said.

She watched him swallow. His throat working over words. His eyes darted here and there, likely searching for an escape.

"I know this isn't a traditional marriage, but—"

"I can't." He swallowed again even harder this time. "Dance, I mean."

Maggie looked down at his covered leg. She felt her face redden. "Oh. I'm sorry. I should've realized ..."

"I'll do it."

Maggie turned to face Xavier. The dark-haired man held out his hand to her. She turned back to Dylan. Her husband's jaw was clenched, but he nodded his permission.

Trying not to appear defeated, Maggie took Xavier's hand and allowed him to twirl her onto the makeshift dance floor which was just a patch of dirt in the picnic area. Xavier whirled and twirled her for one song.

Xavier was replaced by Reed who whirled and twirled her with his steel arm. Fran and Sean lined up beside her to do a coordinated dance. Before she knew it, she was laughing, breathless, and having the best time of her life.

The men surrounded her, accepting her like she was one of them. The dogs nipped at their heels getting in on the fun. It was what Maggie had always dreamed of; she was being welcomed into a group, a clique, a unit as one of them.

Still, every few beats Maggie snuck a peek at Dylan. His eyes never left her. He also never moved closer. Until the moment he was standing in front of her.

The music slowed and the others moved away. Maggie was about to beg off the next dance as well to catch her breath. But with Dylan standing before her, his hand outstretched, her heart sped and her breath quickened.

"We're supposed to have the first dance as husband and wife. I don't want to buck tradition," he said. "We'll take it slow, okay?"

Maggie took his hand and slipped into the circle of his embrace. For the first time in her lonely life, she understood the meaning of the word home. They barely moved, only swayed to the beat.

It didn't matter if they took it slow or not. She had already arrived. She was already in love with this man. And she had a lifetime to wait for him to catch up with her.

CHAPTER SEVENTEEN

S he felt good in his arms. She felt right. So good, so right that after the song ended, he didn't let her go.

When the music stopped, Dylan's hand slid up Maggie's back, tracing her spine. He followed the path of her shoulder blades and on down the span of her forearms until he found the back of her hands. One by one, each of his fingers entwined with hers until their digits were wrapped around each other.

Dylan felt warmth course through his body. The heat shot up his arm, it pooled in his chest and then spread down to his legs. Both of his legs.

A fever replaced the phantom ache in the leg

he'd lost. It was a spark that insisted he could run again. It was a flare that swore he could fly.

Dylan looked down at Maggie. Somehow, they'd moved from the dance floor and were seated at the head of the main picnic table in front of the half-eaten wedding cake. Their clasped hands rested on the bench between them.

Maggie wasn't looking at him. She was feeding a bone to one of her dogs; Stevie, the overweight Rottweiler. He knew the Rottweiler couldn't see him. Still, Stevie's panting mouth split wide, as though he were smiling. His eyes sparkled as though to say, *welcome to my family*.

Dylan's gaze returned to Maggie. She still held his hand, but she leaned her chin on the other and looked across the table, smiling and laughing. His friends gathered around them at the table, regaling Maggie with embarrassing stories about him, asking her about her life.

That raging fire that had grown in Dylan now banked into a steady burn. The men who'd trusted him with their lives and their future had welcomed the woman he'd chosen for his life and future.

They'd accepted her and her dogs. They were all a unit now. Dylan knew that just as the men had each other's backs, they now had Maggie's.

"So you got any girlfriends you could hook me up with?" asked Reed.

Reed was one of the only men excited by the venture of holy matrimony. Dylan knew that Reed wanted a family and a wife to care for. Unlike himself and the other men, Reed was one to not let his very visible wound get in the way.

"I really don't have many girlfriends," said Maggie.

Somehow, Dylan knew that translated to she didn't have *any* girlfriends. Maggie had moved through life alone. At the worst times, she'd been used and abused by the system. That life was over.

"I spend most of my time with animals," she said.

"Then you'll fit in perfectly here," said Fran.

Maggie blushed, but her smile said everything. She was overwhelmed by their acceptance, and he could tell that she was grateful for it. Dylan didn't know where he'd be without these guys. They'd saved his life. That's why he was fighting for theirs. And now that Maggie had taken his hand, they'd all be safe. They could keep this haven they'd found and make it their permanent home.

The sun was setting on this momentous day. Maggie turned to him, and it was as though she were gasoline pulling the flames of the fire inside him high enough to touch the sun. But when she stifled a yawn, the blaze once again cooled. Dylan leaped into protector mode.

"All right guys," he said. "I'm going to take my wife home."

The men made simpering sounds and kissing noises like grade schoolers. Dylan rolled his eyes. He almost opened his mouth to deny what the men were thinking, but then he looked down at Maggie.

Her blush was near crimson now. She knew this wasn't to be a physical marriage. Still, Dylan was certain he caught a spark of desire in her eyes. That's what killed the words on his lips.

Would he never have a physical relationship again in his life? Well, he was married now. So his only option would be with Maggie. He would never dream, never think to go outside of his marriage. But could he possibly perform his duty inside his marriage?

He stood awkwardly. His leg aching from all the activity of the day. He had his answer.

Maggie saw it. He knew she did by the sudden tension in her hand, which he still held. By the quick averting of her gaze.

She said nothing. Instead, she turned and thanked everyone for all they'd done for her special day. Her sincerity rang loud and clear in her words and tone. She bid them all a good night. Then, with a signal to her dogs, she and Dylan headed back to their home.

They walked side by side, slowly. Their fingers were still entwined. Dylan couldn't think of a single thing to say to her, his wife. All he could concentrate on was the feel of her fingers, the brush of her forearm against his.

He thought back to the desire he'd seen in her eyes. And then that kiss that went on longer than he'd planned. That kiss that she hadn't pulled away from. That kiss that which, if he looked at the way her fingertips touched her lips, he had to assume she wanted to continue.

Maggie had wanted to dance with him. She hadn't let go of his hand. She leaned against him now. Maybe this marriage could be more than convenient? Maybe it could be something real?

But then her leg brushed against his, and he froze. He couldn't feel the flesh of her thigh as he felt her fingers and her arm. His prosthetic could feel nothing. Dylan looked down to make sure his pants leg covered the evidence. Seeing that it did, he disentangled his fingers from hers.

They were at the front door of their home. The

door was unlocked as always. They had nothing and no one to fear on the ranch.

He opened the door for her. She hesitated, looking down at the threshold. Then she gave herself a chiding shake before stepping over the threshold and into the house.

The dogs marched in behind them. Four of them rushed to Maggie's bedroom door. One rushed to his. Only the two humans stood in the hall unsure which door to approach.

"It's been a long day," he said.

Maggie nodded, looking up at him. Her lips parted. Her tongue darted out and moistened her lower lip.

Dylan's gaze tracked the movement. His stomach grumbled. His mouth watered. His palms itched. He need only bend his head and he could take another taste of her. He straightened.

"I want to thank you for everything you've done for me and my men," he said. Even to him, his voice sounded formal.

"Of course," she said, just as stiffly. She closed her mouth and crossed her arms over her body.

"Sleep well, Maggie. I'll see you in the morning."

Before she could say anything else, or he could change his mind, Dylan opened his door. Spin rushed in before he shut it firmly closed. Dylan sagged against the frame. One thing he knew for sure was that he wanted Maggie. He wanted her in the way a man wanted a woman.

If he were honest with himself, he'd admit that it went beyond the physical. Maggie Shaw -now Maggie Banks- found a way into his system. The assault was mounting for an attack on his heart. If she got that far, all would be lost.

CHAPTER EIGHTEEN

M aggie hadn't slept well. She'd tossed and turned all night, moving from the right side of the bed to the left. She awoke sore, irritated, and confused.

On the one hand, Dylan had made it clear that this was a marriage of convenience for them both. Then he'd made pretty speeches about taking care of her every need and becoming her family.

On the other hand, he insisted there would be nothing physical between them. Then he kissed her senseless, got jealous anytime another man showed interest. He held her hand and held her close only to leave her at her bedroom door on their wedding night.

Maggie no longer knew which way was up and

which way was down. She did know the way to Dylan's door. She got out of the bed and dressed for the day. Then she opened her door and, preceded by her furry army, she headed for his.

She knocked lightly at first. Then she knocked more firmly with insistence. Maggie had always been a good judge of character, of both animals and dogs. She didn't worry that he'd be upset with her. What she wanted from him was emotion.

She was safe here with Dylan, with these men. More importantly, she had a shot at a real relationship, a real marriage. And she wasn't giving that up.

Dylan was a wounded animal. He'd agreed to some healing here on this ranch, but he needed more. His leg was under control, but there was a deeper, internal wound.

Maggie hadn't had a lot of experience with love for a man, but she was willing to try. God, she wanted to try. She just needed Dylan to get down from his high horse first.

She'd seen the way he'd looked at her last night before turning away at her bedroom door. He'd held her hand, rubbing at the webbing between her fingers as though he wanted to join with her at the root. And then there had been that kiss ...

It had been her first kiss. It had been her only

kiss. As first and only kisses went, it had been the stuff of dreams, the stuff of storybooks. She wanted this story to come off the page. She wanted a shot at the reality.

Maggie knocked again on Dylan's door. The silence coming from the other end let her know he wasn't there. He'd run away from her again.

She trudged down the stairs, dogs following in her wake. Her empty stomach grumbled, demanded attention as her heart continued to ache. She went into the kitchen. On the stove was a stack of pancakes in a sea of fresh cut strawberries.

It was the sweetest, most thoughtful thing anyone had ever done for her. She shoved the pancakes in a Tupperware container and then stormed out of the house.

Indifference, she could handle. Ignoring, she understood. Being used, she was used to.

But this hot and cold, this sweet and then absent, she couldn't do that.

Maggie shut the dogs in the backyard, leaving their food outside and making sure they had plenty of water. Then she went in search of Dylan. She found him in the training arena.

She stopped in her tracks when she saw him struggling to get on his mount. He hefted himself up with this good leg. Then he had to reach over and bend his prosthetic leg to swing over the horse. The balancing act looked treacherous and her every instinct told her to go to him.

She spied Mark on the other side of the horse. Arms crossed, gaze diverted. But Maggie could tell that the man watched Dylan like a hawk ready to swoop in at any sign of danger.

Dylan made a miscalculation. He readjusted his leg. To do so, he had to lift his pants leg, and that's when he saw her.

His face turned horror-stricken. He yanked the material back over his exposed prosthetic. He swung that leg back over the horse and down to the ground. He landed with a nasty sounding thud and winced.

"What are you doing here?" he demanded when he rounded on her.

Maggie jerked back. Her lips parted in surprise at the vehemence in his voice. Her breath caught at the glare in his beautiful blue eyes.

Dylan's upper body caved in on itself. He shut his eyes in a wince and clenched his fist. When his gaze found hers again, he looked ashamed. But it wasn't enough.

Maggie steeled her spine and marched up to him. "I'm your wife. My place is wherever you are."

Dylan turned away from her, likely looking for his escape. Now she was the one who rounded on him.

"In sickness and in health, Dylan. That's what I promised you. I'm not going to shy away because you have an injury."

"I'm not one of your pets to fix, Maggie."

"No, we're partners. That was the deal. But you keep shutting me out. Let me help—"

She reached out her hand, but he yanked his arm away from her. He took an awkward step back with his prosthetic leg.

Maggie cradled her rejected palm in her hand. "Was this all you needed from me then? Just the marriage? You don't want me even as a helpmate?"

He sighed. His blue eyes finally found hers. They implored her to understand. But how could she when he didn't contradict her.

Maggie took a deep breath. The air was filled with the stench of horses and sweat. She nodded at Dylan. Then she turned and walked away.

Indifference, ignoring, and using she was used to. And it seemed it had come back to her again. What else could she conclude when she walked away? Dylan didn't call after her.

CHAPTER NINETEEN

Dylan watched as Maggie walked away from him. Her retreat began as a slow march, that turned into a brisk walk, and finally a run. He couldn't catch up with her if he'd tried, not with his prosthetic. He'd only wind up hobbling after her, embarrassing himself even further. And so he stood still on stiff legs, watching his wife put distance between them because he'd hurt her.

Again.

Spin nosed at his pants leg. The dog looked between Dylan and Maggie's retreating form, then turned back to Dylan. Spin nosed at Dylan's leg again, pushing the fabric into the cold steel of his metal leg.

Spin cocked his head to the side in confusion.

Then the dog let out a sigh, his little head shook left and right from the impact of the harsh air.

Over on the other side of the horse, Mark looked at Dylan with the same look of disappointment. "If you don't run after that woman, you're a complete idiot."

"I can't run after her." Dylan banged his thigh with a closed fist.

"If you truly believe that, then you don't deserve her, and you need to let her go." Mark turned and walked in the other direction.

Spin howled low, as though he were in pain. He looked again between Dylan and the door. When Dylan still didn't budge, the terrier turned and made his way after Maggie, hobbling along at a steady and awkward clip.

The dog had more bravery and gumption than the man. Spin had been trailing after Dylan since he first got here. But he showed his true allegiance now when he turned his back on Dylan.

When Dylan's parents and ex-fiancée had rejected him, they had turned their backs on him with a look of disgust. Maggie had just turned her back on him now. But the expression on her face hadn't been one of disgust. It hadn't even been one of pity. She'd been hurt and disappointed, but mostly hurt.

It had been a long time since Dylan had been in a position to hurt anyone. This last year that he'd been in recovery and rehabilitation, he'd been so busy supporting those around him. The moment someone had tried to care for him, to offer him support, and maybe even love, he'd pushed her away.

The thing was, Maggie hadn't left him because of his leg. She'd insisted it didn't bother her. She'd accepted him in spite of his injury. The reason she'd run from him wasn't because she was disgusted by his external wound. No, she'd become disgusted with him because of his internal wound, the wound he kept inflicting on her.

Dylan was so afraid of her rejection of him, that the moment she got close enough to hurt him, he pushed her away. No, he shoved her away. Hard.

But even worse, her absence only made him crave her more. So the second she was apart from him, he'd do something to bring her back close. Like, make her a stack of peace pancakes. God, he was a bastard.

"I just saw Maggie running out of here," Fran said

as he came into the training area. "What the hell did you do?"

"Stay out of it. It's none of your business."

"Actually, it is my business. It's all of our business."

"We're not getting divorced, so the ranch is safe. I'll fix it."

"You can't think this is about that? You're not that dense."

Dylan didn't answer. He couldn't. He could see it wasn't just a business transaction for her. It was clear she wanted more. It was becoming evident that he did too. But it couldn't be.

"I've seen the way you are around her," Fran continued.

"But she hasn't seen me. Not the real me."

"Is this about your leg? Because you do realize you married a woman who heals animals that would be helpless without her."

Maggie hadn't balked once at the knowledge of his wound. But knowing it and seeing it were two different things.

"The reason this is my business," said Fran, "the reason this is all of our business, is because that woman is now our family. You don't fix this, you keep hurting her, and you'll have this entire unit to contend with."

There was a part of Dylan that wanted to high-five Fran for coming to Maggie's defense. But the shamed part of him kept his hands clenched in fists at his side.

"You have a woman who's opened her heart to you, who accepts you for who you are, but somehow that's not good enough?"

"That's not what it is."

"Then what?"

"*I'm* not good enough. I can't be the man she needs."

"But it looks to me like you're the man she wants."

Dylan closed his eyes. There was no argument he could forge against Fran's words. Still, he couldn't believe them.

Maggie had no angle. She had no agenda. She made no demands, except on his time and attention. Did he wish she'd come after his inheritance?

Money he could spare. Time he had. Attention he could give.

Maggie wanted a piece of his heart. The erratic beating he felt in his chest told him his heart wanted her back. It skipped a beat, making him think that he'd lost the organ, just as he'd lost his leg. He knew the only thing that would fill it.

It was only the phantom pain in his leg that held him back. His stump itched. Both of his legs itched. He itched to move toward her, to run to find her, to bring her to stand next to him.

Dylan began to move toward the exit before he was conscious.

Behind him, he heard Fran cheer, "Hoorah."

Dylan moved faster than he had in months, but it wasn't fast enough to reach her. He turned back into the training area. Fran was standing by holding the reins of the horse.

Dylan took the reins. He hefted himself up and onto the horse. Then he took Fran's hand to steady himself as he swung his straight leg over the horse.

"Don't screw it up this time," Fran called after Dylan as he took off at a gallop.

Dylan couldn't promise that. He'd seen the answers, but he'd been too afraid of the question. Now the only question that remained was was it too late?

CHAPTER TWENTY

There was so much land. Land as far as the eye could see. Maggie could run in any direction that she wanted. The problem was that she desperately wanted to go back in the direction she'd come.

She heard something behind her. Her heart pounded faster as her legs slowed. Had he come after her after all?

Looking over her shoulder she didn't see a big man. She saw nothing on the horizon. But the sound persisted. Looking down, she saw it, Spin wheeling furiously after her.

Maggie stopped. She went to the little dog so that he didn't have to run any farther.

The poor thing. He was panting. His wheelchair

was about to come loose. It wasn't meant for running. But the terrier had come after her.

Maggie scooped him in her arms and squeezed him tight. He gave her cheek a number of licks, as though he were trying to soothe her. It was something. But it wasn't enough.

The only one who could soothe this ache was her husband. But he couldn't bring himself to reach out to her.

Maggie came to the gazebo where she'd been married just the day before. Many of the decorations were still hanging. She steered clear of those memories and headed to the pier. It was a short pier overlooking the small pond.

The water wasn't blue. It looked as though there was a lot of refuse in the waters. Maybe it was run off from somewhere? It was no matter, she wasn't going in. No matter how much she wanted to sink down into the abyss.

What had she gotten herself into?

Dylan's reaction to her just now had been worse than indifference. She knew he cared, but he had let his fear and his shame get in the way of what they could have. He was hurting, wounded, and she knew that she had what it took to heal him if only he'd let her.

But he wouldn't.

Maggie looked up at the sky. That was a mistake. The azure of the sky was the same blue of Dylan's eyes. Now, each time she looked up, she'd be reminded of him.

Everything she'd ever wanted in her life was here on this ranch. A group of people ready to accept her as one of their own. A place for her animals. A job helping other animals. And a man who was kind and considerate and strong. He just had this one flaw. He bolted and lashed out when she got too close to his injury.

Could she spend the rest of her life in the face of his flaw?

She had said for better or worse in her vows. The better was good. It was really good. Could she manage the worse?

She had to. She'd promised. She'd simply have to find more patience until he trusted her.

He wasn't like the other animals she'd worked with. He was a man. Those beasts were notoriously hard to train and control.

She wouldn't put this relationship down. She'd find a way to foster and make this marriage thrive. She wasn't a quitter. But, man, was she tired. She'd rest here a bit and then go back for the next round.

Maggie closed her eyes and let the healing rays of the sun seep into her skin. When she caught her breath and felt a bit more rejuvenated, she gathered herself together and prepared herself to jump back into the fight. That's when she heard the splash.

She looked beside her to see that Spin was nowhere in sight. The waters of the pond rippled. Oh no. He'd fallen in.

But then he surfaced. His little nose spewing water, his paws swiping at the surface. Maggie leaned over the edge of the pier to grab him. He was too far.

Maggie had never learned to swim. But that didn't matter, not when a life was on the line. Spin's head dipped back below the water's surface. His legs paddled, but the wheelchair weighed him down. His head sunk below the surface again and resurfaced a second later.

Maggie scooted further out. She almost had him. Just one more inch ... and she was in the water.

She was submerged before she'd even taken a breath. The water came at her from all sides. But in front of her was the dog. She reached her arms out and pulled Spin to her.

She kicked and punched, but the water still held

her. They were going to die out here, on a ranch full of heroes, with no one coming to their rescue.

CHAPTER TWENTY-ONE

D ylan pushed the horse harder than he ever had in training. In pushing the horse, he pushed his wounded leg. The ache was very real this time. But he pulled on his training and sucked it up. The pain would be tenfold if he didn't get to Maggie in time before she left him for good.

He pulled the horse to a stop. Pausing to look around. The vastness of the ranch spread out before him. Which direction had she gone?

In the distance, he spied the gazebo where they had been married just the other day. She'd looked up at him with such trust, with such hope, and he'd dashed all of her dreams. He'd give anything to have her look up at him again like that.

The sound of splashing tore him from his

reverie. Dylan turned to the pond beyond the gazebo. Those waters weren't the cleanest, definitely not safe for swimming. It was on their long list of repairs for the ranch, but because most of the men didn't like to show off parts of their body, a swimming hole wasn't a high priority.

There was another splash. Then a pitiful bark, followed by a strangled cry. Had one of Maggie's dogs fallen in the water? With their injuries, they might not be able to swim. Dylan took off toward the lake.

He arrived to see Spin's head coming up out of the water. The dog coughed and spurted, paddling his front legs but moving nowhere. It looked odd that the dog was raising up so high. Then he realized, it was Maggie raising the dog. She must have dived in to save the dog not concerning herself with her own safety and livelihood.

He knew the dog couldn't swim with the apparatus on its leg. How the dog came to be in the water, he had no idea. But Dylan knew the added weight would only let the dog sink. And sink he did when the hands holding him up slipped down in the water.

But why wasn't Maggie surfacing? Was she

caught on something in the water? Couldn't she swim?

Dylan didn't wait to find out. He dismounted. Crashing to the ground, he felt the impact of his hard landing all the way up his stump, but it didn't compare to the pounding in his heart.

He moved faster than he knew he could down the short pier. Neither dog nor woman had surfaced again in over a minute. Was he too late? Too late to save her life? Too late to win her back?

Diving in that water, he knew the moisture would wreck his prosthetic. He also knew the waters could get into his stump and cause an infection. He didn't hesitate at the pier's edge. He leaped in.

Opening his eyes under the water, he saw nothing but bleakness and blackness. He kicked with his good leg, the prosthetic weighing him down.

He reached out his hands and felt nothing but more murky water. But he didn't give up. He couldn't give up. Not on Maggie.

She'd kept coming back to him, even after every time he'd pushed her away. When he'd tried to put distance between them, she'd step just a bit closer. She'd never felt she belonged anywhere or to anyone. He'd offered her a home and a family, but he'd put a door between them, he'd crossed his arms over his heart, he'd walked away from her.

No more. Not ever again.

Dylan reached out to her, determined to find her and pull her into the safety of his heart.

His hands met with fur. Then flesh. He grabbed them both to him and gave a powerful kick with his good leg. When he did, the prosthetic came off, freeing him to make his way up.

He felt lighter as he kicked them all to the surface. They broke the surface with a mighty gasp.

"Hold onto me," Dylan said when he'd taken air into his lungs.

"I can't let Spin go," said Maggie.

"One hand on Spin, one hand on me. I'll get us to the pier."

Maggie did as he instructed. He wrapped one arm around her and kicked with all his might to get them to safety.

Once they reached the pier, Maggie handed Spin onto the pier. The wheelchair had fallen from his small body. Only his two stumps remained. Spin collapsed in a sodden heap on the wood of the pier.

Dylan made sure Maggie's hands were braced on the pier. Then he boosted her up. The water weighed her down, and she made it clumsily onto the pier.

When it was Dylan's turn, he was dead tired. His limbs cried from exertion. But, with great effort, he hefted himself out of the water as well.

He collapsed on the pier, soaked and exposed. Not just his body, but his heart, his soul.

Dylan's and Maggie's gazes connected. Maggie looked him up and down. It took everything in him to hold still while she looked at his missing leg.

But he did it. He held still for her. No more hiding.

Her gaze slid over him, and then her hands followed. Her movements quick and efficient, not a caress or affectionate.

"Are you hurt?" she asked.

A laugh escaped Dylan. At first, it sounded like a cough as he freed a bit of pond water from his chest. Then the laughter rolled out of him like fresh waves. Of course, that would be her first concern.

"Yes," he said after he sobered. "I'm hurt."

Maggie's brows went up in alarm. Before she could move into action, he caught her hands. He brought himself up to a sitting position so that he could look her in her eyes.

"I am a hurt and wounded creature," he said. "Not

the kind to lash out, the kind to hide away so others won't see and pity him."

"I don't pity you," she said.

"No, you don't." He ran the backs of his fingers down the side of her face. He'd just come so close to losing her. If he hadn't have followed after her she might be dead. He brought her into his arms, holding her so close he felt her heart beating.

"I don't pity you," she said again. "I love you."

Dylan pulled back to peer into her face. What he saw sent a rush of emotion through him that was so powerful it nearly knocked him on his back.

"I know that wasn't part of the deal," she said, averting her gaze. "But I couldn't help it. Despite your stubbornness, and your infuriating need for independence and self-reliance, you have the biggest heart of any person I've ever met. You are so selfless in how you take care of others. I want to be the one to take care of you."

"Okay." It was the only word that he could get past his constricted throat. Just those two syllables.

"Okay?"

"I want that," he nodded. "I want all of that. I want you. I want all of you. Not just on paper. I've felt like half a man for so long, but you make me feel whole. I'm a whole man when I'm with you."

Maggie looked up at him and beamed. Her face was full of trust and hope. Dylan's heart lurched for her. And then he was pulling her close.

Their lips met under the sun's gentle rays. The water had chilled him, but the press of her lips to his warmed him through. He pulled her tighter into his embrace to offer her everything that he had to give.

"I love you, too," he said when they broke apart.

"You do?"

"I do."

She swallowed, choking back tears, but one escaped her right eye. "No one's ever said that to me before."

"I'll say it every day from now on." Dylan wiped the solitary tear away. When he did, another fell. "I'll say it so much you'll grow tired of hearing it."

"I don't think that's possible."

"Let's see."

He pulled her in for another kiss, but before their lips could meet they were both showered with a spray of water as Spin shook the excess water from his coat.

Maggie and Dylan laughed at the little dog's antics. Spin stood tall on his two front legs, entirely unconcerned and unfazed about his appearance.

Maggie's hand fell away from Dylan's shoulder and landed on his stump.

He waited for instinct to kick in and cause him to jerk from her touch. That instinct never showed up. Instead, he covered her hand with his. Their fingers entwined as both their palms rested on the wound that no longer ached.

"We need to get you both back to the ranch and clean those wounds," Maggie said. "You both are at risk for infection."

Dylan scooped the dog into his arms. "This is one brave dog."

"He's the reason we're together. If I hadn't have saved his life, I wouldn't have lost my job and found my way here."

"Seems like this rescued dog, rescued us."

"Yeah," Maggie agreed, giving the terrier a little scratch behind the ears.

Then she looked up at Dylan. They both did. Spin with trust in his gaze. Maggie with love in hers. Maggie ran her hand down Dylan's face, and he melted into her touch. Spin settled between them as their lips met again.

EPILOGUE

Four little dogs nipped around Fran's heels as they all made their way from Dylan and Maggie's backyard to the front of the house. Fran walked slowly and carefully so as not to step on any tails or feet or prosthetics.

The dogs were all excited to see their masters returned from the hospital where Dylan had spent a few days to treat an infection he'd acquired after jumping into the pond to save Maggie and her little terrier, or the Little Terror as Fran had christened him. The little dog followed Fran everywhere in Dylan's absence.

The dog was clearly in need of a leader to suck up to. That could never be Fran. Fran didn't have time to lead anyone. He meant that as a literal statement. His days were numbered and everyone knew it.

Fran looked back in the yard, noting that the fifth dog had yet to make his way over. Sugar, the Golden Retriever, sat under the shade of a tree. The sleeping dog opened one eye and then gave a sigh as he slowly got to his feet and trudged over. The poor dog had diabetes, a manageable disease, but the dog needed insulin treatments, and he was constantly thirsty and sleepy. Fran made sure to give the dog an extra pat. He and the dog had formed a bit of a friendship since Sugar couldn't always keep up with his doggy siblings.

Fran understood not being able to keep up with the pack. When he was up on a horse, he wanted to push the great beast to gallop, but knew it wasn't the best thing for his own health condition. So he kept to a light canter at most on his rides, which never left him satisfied. Fran waited for Sugar to join him, then the two made their way out the back gate.

At the front of the house, Reed and Sean sat rocking in porch chairs. The dogs wound about their legs. Reed pulled the tiny Chihuahua, Soldier, who'd lost his front left arm, onto his lap. Sean gave Stevie, the partially blind dog, a scratch behind the ear. In the distance, they could see Maggie's truck make the turn into the ranch and begin down the long road toward the living quarters.

"You really gonna give up living on the ranch?" Reed asked Sean.

"Don't really have much choice," said Sean. "No woman will want to marry me with a mug like this."

"If you're fishing for a compliment, Jeffries, you won't find one here," said Reed.

"I'm serious," Sean rolled his eyes. He wasn't wearing his sunshades today as they were the only ones around him. The deep gashes on his face added to the frown he gave Reed. "I look like a monster."

"So, you're headed home?" asked Fran. He knew the answer to the question though.

Sean shook his head. "I'll figure something out. We still got two months before the new paperwork gets filed."

Fran had options. They just weren't any that he liked. He'd rather stay here with his friends and be surrounded by those that cared about him for his last days. However long they were. But he knew the shrapnel that lay dangerously close to his heart could move at any minute. How could he offer his heart to any woman under that threat?

The truck pulled to a stop in front of the home.

Dylan stepped out of the truck, leaning on Maggie. He wore shorts, exposing his prosthetic leg.

"Aw man, Mags," moaned Reed. "You brought him back alive?"

"Sorry," she grinned. "It was unavoidable. The hospital was very eager to release him."

"What did he do?" asked Fran. He knew his friend wasn't the best patient.

"Let's just say, nurses don't respond well to commands," Maggie said.

"You will note that no one said I was wrong," Dylan grumbled as they came up the steps.

Dylan leaned down to Maggie's upturned face and planted a soft kiss at the corner of her mouth. The two gazed at each other as though no one was there. Until the dogs began to bark for attention.

Maggie and Dylan broke apart with a grin and looked down at their brood. Ears were scratched, heads were patted as they all made their way into the house.

"You guys coming in for dinner?" asked Maggie.

"Depends on who's cooking," said Reed.

"Hey!" She reached back and gave him a punch on his shoulder.

The punch elicited a chuckle from Reed. Dylan

pointed to his chest to indicate that he'd be the one doing the cooking. They all loved Maggie. She was great as a healer and a friend, but cooking was not her strong suit.

Dogs and humans filed into the front door, full of energy and life. Fran kept step with Sugar who made slow progress up the stairs. Once on the porch, the dog needed to rest a moment before heading inside with the rest of his family.

So, Fran waited a few moments with the dog until they both caught their breath. Their illnesses might slow them down, but it wouldn't keep them from their goals. Sugar's goal was to get to the offering in his doggie dish and then pal around with his pack. Fran's goals were somewhat similar.

He wanted to break bread with his fellow soldiers. But more importantly, Fran wanted to make sure his pals were all situated on the ranch for as long as they wanted to remain. And that would mean Fran would have to find each of them a bride in two months.

If he was still on this earth after that, he could visit the ranch on weekends and holidays. He'd watch his friends flourish in this place that had given them all back their lives after combat had scarred them. But the ranch could only heal Fran so much.

With a sigh, Sugar got back to his feet and took the steps to cross the threshold into the house. Fran understood; being sick sucked. It kept you from the things you wanted most in life, the things you once dreamed of and now insisted you didn't want because they were out of your reach.

A good man like Fran,
who puts those he cares about before himself,
is destined to find a woman to heal his ravaged heart.

Watch him fall hopefully in love in
"Hand Over His Heart"
the second book in The Brides of Purple Heart Ranch!

Turn the page for a sneak peek!

If you'd like to be a part of Shanae's Readers group
please sign up at
http://bit.ly/PurpleHeartBrides

A scholar reaching for her dreams. A hero living on borrowed time. Can she make them a permanent arrangement before his time runs out?

Francisco DeMonti has always been a man with a plan. Though his last plan led to his entire squad being wounded on a mission in Afghanistan. Now he's seeking redemption by getting all the men in his unit hitched so they can stay together and heal on the Purple Heart Ranch. But his own heart is under lock and key due to the shrapnel around it that could kill him at any moment.

Eva Lopez has always believed in the power of education. After years of scraping and saving, she finally steps foot onto a college campus only to be yanked away by the mean streets she came from. A local gang threatens her family's safety until a wounded veteran offers a reprieve: marry a soldier in exchange for protection and the freedom to attend school.

Fran has every intention of directing Eva towards one of his brothers in arms, men who aren't in danger of a sudden death, but he can't resist the brainy brunette and proposes to her himself. He'll protect for as long as he breathes, but falling in love is futile for a man with a ticking time bomb in his chest. Eva can't help falling for the man who is making her dreams come true, but when he keeps her at arm's length, can she convince him to make this marriage more than a convenience no matter how much or how little time they have left?

Find out if love can truly heal all wounds in this light-hearted, sweet romance of convenient arrangements that unfold into lasting love. *Hand Over His Heart* is the second in a series of marriage of convenience tales featuring Wounded Warriors who are healed with the power of love.

Here's an excerpt of the book!

Chapter One

Fran watched the blip on the monitor. It spiked high as though traversing the tallest peak and instantly fell low like a man with a failed parachute. Only to rise and do it again.

If that wasn't a metaphor for his life, he wouldn't know what was.

He watched the EKG monitor as his heart beat a few more times. The pulsing was strong, consistent. For now. But just as the doctor monitoring his heart knew, Fran knew that the beating could stop at any moment.

"Looks like there's no change, Corporal DeMonti." Dr. Nelson's voice was steady, monochromatic like the blipping on the screen he watched. He scribbled notes on a pad with a pencil, looking from one machine, to another, to his watch. Not once at Fran.

Fran was used to being overlooked by those who thought they were superior to him. As a Corporal in the U.S. Army, he'd striven to a higher rank. He'd been a heartbeat away from advancing to Sergeant. Until one mission went terribly wrong.

So, no, the doctor's lack of attentiveness didn't bother him. What did was the fact that the man wrote with a pencil instead of a pen. The graphite touching down on the page was impermanent to Fran. It could be wiped out with the pink eraser on the other end. Just as Fran's life could be wiped out with the wrong move. If the shrapnel that had lodged itself in his chest moved a few millimeters to the left and punctured his heart he would be erased from existence. Gone from the page of life.

"Unfortunately, it's still too dangerous to go in and remove it," said the doctor. He looked up and faced Fran finally. "All we can do is keep up with your therapy and pray."

It always shocked Fran when he heard a doctor prescribe prayer. He would think that most of the scientifically minded men and women would prefer the tangible instead of the spiritual. But he was often wrong. At least he was in the veteran's hospital. Many of the men and women here had been in and gotten out of situations that could only be attributed to a higher power. So, they didn't shy away from calling on the Lord when their minds couldn't solve a physical problem.

Fran knew full well that his best bet at life was the Lord. So, he had no problem taking the medicine prescribed. He just wished he knew the Lord's plan more clearly. Did He want Fran to come home to him soon? Or was his will to let Fran stay out and play for a while?

Fran preferred having a solid plan. But he also knew the old adage; Man plans and God laughs.

He didn't think God was laughing at him. He wouldn't allow himself to believe that the Creator would make such a cruel joke.

As Fran left the exam room, a few of the women in the halls smiled at him, trying to catch his eye. To the naked eye, Fran looked entirely healthy. He hadn't lost a limb or gained any visible scars, except on his chest. No, his wound was deep. Past the metal in his chest. This wound went down into his soul.

It was all his fault.

Fran and his squad had been doing work to improve the lives of women and children when it happened. The blast that put shrapnel in Fran's chest hadn't taken any lives. But it had taken away six livelihoods, plus the human bomber who'd sacrificed his life for a misguided calling.

For the survivors, their lives were forever changed. And just when they were all getting their lives back on track at the Bellflower Ranch, another bomb had exploded in their lives. No, this couldn't possibly be a joke. It was all too cruel.

Fran pulled out of the vet hospital and headed across town to the ranch. His heart swelled as he looked out at the scenery before him. Colorado was simply beautiful.

Fran had grown up in New York City. His mountains had been skyscrapers. His fields had been asphalt. But there was nothing like seeing the beauty and majesty of nature rise up into the sky.

Afghanistan had had the same effect on him. In a place described as a desert, there had been rugged mountains and deep valleys. Snow topped the jagged peaks. The valleys were fertile for crops and livestock.

He'd been shocked to find beauty and bounty in a place portrayed as vile. But that portrait did not include everyone in its frame. The good people of the country tried to keep out of the picture. Very often, they were unsuccessful and the brush stroke of violence colored their lives.

Fran pulled up to the ranch. When his squad leader had purchased the ranch, the soldiers quickly renamed it The Purple Heart Ranch. The lush, violet leaves of a bellflower looked like the emblem of the same name. The Purple Heart was awarded to those who served in combat and were wounded by enemy hands. Each man in his squad had been wounded, and now that they'd come here to heal, they'd been dealt another blow.

Fran and the men of his squad had to get married in a matter of weeks if they all wanted to stay on the ranch that had begun to heal their wounds and had given them back their purposes. The problem was there weren't many women who would want to be shackled for life to a group of wounded warriors. Definitely not one who couldn't give his heart because it could stop beating at any moment.

So, Fran would need to leave the ranch soon. But not before he saw that the rest of the men were settled. Since he'd been responsible for them all losing a part of themselves, he owed them that much. He'd make sure they'd all have the security they deserved. And who knew, maybe they'd even find love.

It was a nice dream. One he'd once had for himself. But it was one he knew he'd never have since his chest was a ticking time bomb.

Chapter Two

Eva took a deep, steadying breath. Still, her fingers shook. She lifted the pen off the slip of paper, shook out her fingers, and tried again.

She did the math mentally in her head. She couldn't make a mistake writing the numerals and their corresponding amount in words. This was a big check. The biggest she'd ever written in her life.

After triple checking, and then triple checking again, she put the pen down. It rolled away from her, but she let it. She didn't need the ink any longer. The money was spent, and her account was now empty. But it was worth it.

She carefully tore the check from the book. It was check number one. She had never written one before. She'd always paid in cash. This was her first checking account that was used to write and not cash checks. And this was her first check.

She handed it over to the woman behind the counter. Her eyes were kind, and her smile patient. She looked over the check.

Eva held her breath. She couldn't have made a mistake. She couldn't afford another dime to be squeezed into that check.

"Everything looks good, my dear," said the woman.

Eva's shoulders visibly dropped at the confirmation.

"Here's your schedule." The admissions representative handed Eva a half sheet of paper with room numbers, class names, and professors printed in neat lines. "We'll see you on Monday, Ms. Lopez."

"Yes," Eva breathed "Yes, you will."

"Enjoy your classes, sweetheart."

"You, too. I mean, thank you. Enjoy your day."

Eva turned from the admissions window clutching the schedule to her chest. Behind her, the line of students aiming to register was long. They looked bored and tired. None had the excitement in their veins that she had. Likely because most of them had scholarships, or financial aid, or parents to pay for their education.

Not Eva. She'd earned every penny she'd just signed over to the school. It had taken her three years, but she'd done it. She'd saved enough for her first semester of college. Not online. She was going to an actual campus. And not a few community college classes. This was a state university.

She wasn't being a snob. Well, actually she was. For the first time in her life, she was part of the elite class. She just wished her parents could see her now. Somehow, she knew they were looking down on her and beaming with pride.

She'd done it. She'd made her dream come true. Her parents had told her from the first day of kindergarten; education was the key to her dreams. With schooling, anything was possible.

Eva didn't know exactly what she wanted to do with her education. She only knew that she wanted one. She loved being in school, sitting behind a desk while the teacher worked magic on a whiteboard.

These last three years since graduating from high school had been dreary. But soon, she'd be back behind a desk where she belonged. Then, anything was possible.

Eva hopped on the city bus and began the trek home. Home was beyond the nice neighborhoods surrounding the college. Home was beyond the trendy apartment complexes in the business district. Home was a rundown complex in the less than trendy part of town where people worked hourly wages that were often below the state minimum.

The bus didn't get close to her complex. It let Eva off at the church. She'd come to this church a few times in the past few months since she'd been living here. Wherever Eva moved, she always made sure to find a church. Even if she didn't know anyone, church was always home.

"Good afternoon, Ms. Lopez."

Eva turned at the sound of the older man's voice. A smile broke across her face. "Hello, Pastor Patel."

Eva went over and shook the man's hand. He brushed that away and gave her a hearty hug. Eva accepted it gratefully. Pastor Patel gave the kind of hugs her father used to give.

"I haven't seen you for a couple of weeks," Pastor Patel admonished her.

"I picked up a few extra shifts to earn money. But you'll see me now. I'll have more time on the weekends. I've done it. I've enrolled in college."

"Oh, my dear, I'm thrilled for you." He rubbed her shoulder affectionately like her mother always did. "Still, I wish you had taken the church funds."

Eva shook her head. In addition to the need for a good education, Eva's father had also impressed on her that they didn't take charity. They worked for everything that came to them. Give to the church and the less fortunate. For the rest, they relied on family. That was the Lopez way of life.

"Well, now that you're a college woman," said Pastor Patel, "you'll come and give a talk to the youth group tomorrow?"

Eva hesitated. She wasn't sure she had anything to teach anyone yet. She had trouble getting her own siblings to listen to her advice for life. She knew Pastor Patel wouldn't take no for an answer. So, she agreed. With one final hug, he let her go on her way.

Eva walked briskly down the street. It was evident why the bus didn't go into her neighborhood. There was glass on the street. Stench came from some alleys. Men lounged on the street corners in the afternoon before the end of the workday. One of those men was a little too short to be considered a man.

"Carlos," Eva called.

The boy didn't turn, but she knew he heard her.

Eva marched up to her brother. She stopped short of yanking up the pants sagging around his bottom. Where was the belt she'd bought him last month? He turned to her with wary eyes. The guys around him began to snicker.

"I was just hanging with my friends," he said.

"Well, it's time to come and do your homework."

The boys snickered some more.

"Go with your fine sister, little man. When you're done with that school work, I got some real work for you."

Eva cut the thug with her eyes. But the Evil Eye only worked on blood relations.

Carlos came with his sister. She knew she'd embarrassed him. But better those boys think he's a mama's boy or sister's boy. She'd ruin his reputation if it meant he'd be saved from the streets.

"Hanging on the streets won't get you anywhere," she said once they'd crossed the street.

"And school will? Look where it's got you." Carlos raised his hands to indicate the neighborhood. All she could see was various shades of brown, from the buildings to the dirt on the streets to the dirt on the kids' faces.

"This is going to change soon," said Eva. "A college degree is a way out of here. You'll see."

The problem was it would take at least two years to show him the truth of her logic. She just hoped she had that much time to prove her point. In the meantime, she would not let the streets claim her baby brother.

Chapter Three

Fran parked his truck in front of his place. It was a

four-bedroom bungalow nestled in the corner of the land. He'd set up shop here when he'd arrived. He'd been the first to arrive a year ago after they were all discharged. He'd assumed they'd all stay in there, but as the men came to the ranch still suffering from their pains, they each sought out their own space.

Dylan took the two-bedroom cottage next to Fran's. Reed, Sean, and Xavier each settled into the small row houses at the end of the road.

Fran looked up at the place he'd called home for a year. It was a comfortable home, but too big for him. He supposed one of the other guys would move in once they found their brides. Hell, maybe they'd even start families and fill the rooms.

That was yet another dream that Fran wouldn't see come to light. He couldn't fathom bringing a child into this world. Not when he wouldn't be around to care for him, to see her grow, or to leave his wife alone with all of his responsibilities. He wasn't built that way.

He'd have to start packing up soon. But not today. Today, he just needed to check on the other guys and make sure they were on track to matrimony which would secure their stays on the ranch.

The door to Dylan's house opened. Barks and yips spilled over the threshold before any humans did. The first over the threshold was Star, a pug with patches of skin missing from her back. The dog had a tendency to walk sideways, as though she didn't want others to see her imperfections.

On her tail was Stevie, a partially blind Rottweiler with a beautiful grayish-blue coat. The dog kept his nose close to Star to guide his way.

Sugar, the Golden Retriever, made slow work out of the door. His head perked up when he sensed Fran. Fran's spirit lightened at the sight of the dog. Dog and man made their way to each other. From all outer appearances, Sugar looked like a healthy dog. But the retriever had diabetes which slowed him down from time to time.

Fran bent down and gave the dog's head a good rub. The two had taken to each other the past few weeks the dogs had been there. Diabetes in dogs was rough, but not the end of the line. Maggie, Dylan's wife, took care of all her wounded dogs. Watching her had shown the soldiers that their wounds weren't impediments to love.

"You're back."

Fran looked up to find Dylan coming down the porch steps of his home. He held a dog in his arms. Spin, an Irish Terrier, had lost his hind legs a few weeks ago. Dylan put the dog down and attached a wheelchair apparatus to his hindquarters.

As Dylan straightened, Fran caught sight of the man's own prosthetic leg. It was an unusual sight. Dylan usually kept his legs covered with long pants to hide his injury. But since getting married and finding acceptance for who he was, he'd begun wearing shorts and cargo pants, letting his prosthetic shine.

"How'd it go?" Dylan asked. "What did the doctor say?"

Before Fran could answer, Maggie poked her head out of the door. All of the dogs turned to her, tails wagging and tongues lagging. Dylan turned to her as well. His tongue didn't fall out of his mouth, but his grin spread wide.

"Hon, don't forget Sugar's medicine when you go into town."

Dylan scooped his wife into his arms. He planted a kiss at the space between her cheek and her nose. Maggie smiled into the embrace. Her head turned and her gaze landed on Fran.

Fran had meant to look away, but his eyes soaked up the affection that he would likely never have for himself.

"Fran, you're back," said Maggie. "What did the

doctor say? Is there any change?"

This was the other reason why Fran couldn't be in a relationship. Maggie wasn't even his partner, yet she had hope in her eyes. Hope that he'd miraculously be cured. It was an unlikely chance that would ever happen. He was lucky just to be alive.

Fran shook his head and braced himself for their compassion and goodwill efforts.

"I've got a lead on some specialists," said Dylan. "We'll go take a visit."

"I'll keep praying for you," said Maggie. "We're not giving up."

Sugar rubbed up against Fran's side. He leaned down and gave the dog his attention as his friends continued to try in vain to save his life.

"In the meantime," Dylan said, "you need to get looking for a bride. We're running out of time if we all want to stay on the ranch."

Fran hadn't bothered arguing. Dylan outranked him and would have no problem giving orders. Though this was an order Fran would not feel compelled to follow. So, instead, he nodded and changed the direction of the conversation.

"Reed said he was having success finding women through a dating app," he said.

"It's a crazy idea," said Dylan. "But desperate times, desperate measures. Right?"

"I'll catch you guys later." Fran turned to leave. Sugar trailed in his wake. Fran turned back to Maggie. "Is it okay if he tags along?"

"Of course," Maggie smiled. "Just don't let him get too excited. And watch that he doesn't eat anything he's not supposed to."

"I know the drill," Fran assured the dog's owner.

He and the dog took off down the path. The ranch sprawled out around them. He saw Xavier riding one of the therapy horses. The horses helped strengthen limbs lost, but just the feel of being atop a horse gave a man back his sense of power. Fran's day to ride was tomorrow. He wished he could go faster than a trot. But with his condition, he had to be careful.

Instead of riding hard, Fran spent a lot of his time in the gardens. Working the soil was good exercise for the body, but also the mind. Watching things grow under his care soothed his soul.

"Fran, wait up," Reed called out to him.

Reed came from the mess hall of the big house where they ate many of their meals together, even though each bungalow had its own kitchen. Reed waved a phone in his good hand. The sleeve of his shirt was rolled up and pinned to the shoulder of his shirt where the forearm had gone missing, left behind on a blast back in Afghanistan.

"Look at this." Reed shoved a cell phone in front of Fran's nose. "Fifty responses so far."

On the screen was a carousel of images of women. Doctor Patel had told them about the app. It was designed by one of the psychologist's relatives. Patel had a hand in the compatibility algorithm.

"Are these all women who want to meet you?" Fran asked.

"Not just meet me. They want to marry me. And we thought this would be hard." Reed cradled his phone in his palm, swiping left and right with his thumb. Not much slowed the man down or got the man down much less a missing limb.

"Marry you? Complete strangers want to marry you? Do they know about ... you know?"

Reed clicked over to his profile picture. It showed him clearly. He was in uniform with a missing arm. "Only thing a woman loves more than a man in a uniform? A wounded soul she thinks she can heal."

Fran sighed. Not because Reed was being a jerk. Fran knew the man expected to find his true love out of this ordeal. Reed was optimistic to a fault.

"This app matches compatibility to ninety-nine

percent. If I can't find my life partner here, then she doesn't exist. I've narrowed it down to these five. This one has a ninety-eight percent match."

Reed held up a picture of a pretty woman. The photo was staged, like she was a model. She was blonde with light green eyes but a touch too much make-up for Fran's liking.

"She's practically perfect," he said. "I've invited her out for drinks this weekend. But she's out of town until the end of the month."

Fran wasn't sure what to say. He wasn't sure if Reed was off his list of soldiers to watch, or if he'd need to keep an even closer eye on the guy to ensure his future was truly set. Fran was determined that all of the men would be settled and able to stay on the ranch after he was gone. Maybe this arranged marriage thing was something, especially if everyone knew what they were getting into beforehand.

Reed continued on, telling Fran more of the woman's attributes. But Fran's attention was else-where. Sean Jeffries came down the steps of the medical offices. It was a converted barn they used for Dr. Patel and the nurses and other personnel who attended them and the therapy animals. Sean held the door open, making sure to turn his head so that only his good side was presented to those who came out.

Out came Ruhi Patel, Dr. Patel's daughter. Ruhi was a nurse and often came to help her father with the soldiers that lived on and visited the ranch for their care.

Ruhi and Patel chattered as they came down the steps. Sean looked down at the ground. But Fran saw him sneaking glances at Nurse Ruhi.

Fran sighed. He'd long suspected Sean had a thing for Ruhi. If he did, Sean wouldn't consent to finding a bride on a dating app. That would mean Sean would be leaving the ranch too.

Dr. Patel looked up, spotting the other men. He waved them over.

"I see you're using the app," Patel said to Reed.

"I have a date next week with a seventy-two percent match," said Reed, holding up his phone to showcase a brunette with a round face. Looked like he'd forgotten all about the ninety-eight percent model.

"I think it's criminal what they're forcing you all to do," said Ruhi. "Forcing you to marry to keep your home."

"I thought you believed in arranged marriage," said Reed.

"This is forced marriage. That's illegal."

"No one's forcing us," said Reed. "We don't have to if we don't want to. We can live somewhere else and come here for our treatment."

Sean looked away. Fran knew the man didn't have anywhere else to go which meant there was force in his situation. Fran didn't want to go either. He loved waking up on the ranch. But he didn't have a choice. His heart wouldn't let him stay.

"My father's been trying to match me since I was a teenager," said Ruhi. "I have no interest in arranged marriages. I don't think I ever want to get married. There's no need in this day and age."

The way Sean's throat worked told Fran that the guy was beyond liking Ruhi and was likely full blown in love. This would be a problem.

"What about you, Francisco?" asked Dr. Patel. "Are you in the market for a bride?"

"I can't give my heart away. It's broken."

He'd said it with a smile, hoping to get a laugh. No one did. They all knew his condition.

"It's a cliché, but they say love heals wounds," said Dr. Patel.

Fran wanted to say love couldn't move metal, but he held his tongue and nodded.

"If you're not ready for love, perhaps you can

spend some time inspiring the next generation? It's Youth Day tomorrow at the church. I have a feeling your insights, especially your belief in a good education, could enlighten some young souls."

Chapter Four

Eva and Carlos climbed the steps to their apartment. It was a three flight walk up. On the ground floor, one of the neighbors had aluminum covering the holes of her screen doors. There were more patches of dirt than grass in what barely passed for a yard.

The heavy glass security door required a key to enter. But as always, it was propped open so that anyone could gain access. Eva didn't bother moving the box from propping up the doorway. She knew that as soon as the door closed shut, someone else would prop something else in the entry.

She climbed the steps with her brother in tow. Bugs skittered out of their way. Off in the corner, a rodent looked up at them as though annoyed that their footfalls had disturbed its peace.

They reached their door and Eva produced a set of keys. She set about unlocking the three sets of bolts before the door gave way, but only a little. The chain link was on.

"Rosalee," Eva called between the chain.

There was rustling inside. Then the pad of socked feet on the worn wooden floors. Without socks, splinters were an issue.

Brown eyes appeared in the slit of the door. Then it closed. There was a rustle of chain and the door came open, but only wide enough to let the two bodies in. Then a slam and the clanking of all the locks being put back into place.

"You have a good day at school, Rosalee?"

Rosalee shrugged. Her skin was pale. She was lanky instead of plump from her inactivity. Eva knew her sister needed to get out more, or she wouldn't develop better social skills. But inside was safe, so she didn't argue much.

"Got an A on my science paper," said Rosalee, "but a B on my English paper. I'm revising it now to resubmit next week."

Eva nodded. Her sister believed in schoolwork to exclusion of going out and being sociable. Her brother preferred to spend his time outside rather than in the classroom. If she could just merge them together, she'd have the perfect kid.

Carlos went to the fridge. From here, Eva could

see it was pretty bare. Things would be hard for a few weeks while she got settled in class. She should be hearing back from the student worker program soon. In the meantime, it would be Ramen every night for a while.

"Aunt Val is in her room with her boyfriend." Rosalee headed back to the room Eva shared with both her younger siblings in the cramped two-bedroom apartment.

Aunt Val had taken them in last year after Uncle Ricardo had his son come back to live with them. Before that, they'd stayed with some distant cousins, but that neighborhood was worse than this one, and Eva had quickly moved them out. Aunt Val's daughter had left the state with her boyfriend, and Eva had jumped on getting her room. Val had lived there for years, which meant there would be some stability.

Giggles and heavy breathing came from her aunt's closed door. Stability was a relative term. Her aunt had a revolving door of men coming and going, but she'd stayed put in that apartment for ten years. Eva just needed her to stay for two more years, and then she would be able to afford her own place with a college degree and job prospects.

All Eva needed was two years—three tops—

before she had her degree secured, a job in the career she chose and moved her family into their own three-bedroom home.

Eva went to the kitchen to prepare the Ramen just as her aunt's bedroom door opened. The burly boyfriend of the week spilled out. He gave Eva a once over that lingered a little too long. Eva kept her gaze averted. She didn't need any trouble with this man.

"Oh, Eva, you're back. I have great news."

Val was in her early forties, but she looked a bit older. She'd had a hard life, raising three kids and losing two of them to the streets.

"You'll never guess." Aunt Val held out her finger. There was a worn, faded-silver band on her fourth finger with a speck of a diamond. One gem was missing. "I'm getting married. Mike proposed. Can you believe it? At my age. I'm getting married."

Eva's hand stilled on the pot she'd just filled with water. "Wow. That's great." Though you couldn't tell from her tone. "So, Mike will be moving in here?"

Mike grimaced. "No. I'm taking my bride and moving her in with me."

Eva gulped. She turned a mutinous glare on her once stable aunt. "You're leaving?"

"Yes, but you can have the apartment all to yourself."

"I can't afford this apartment on my own."

Aunt Val frowned. "Sure you can. Your job pays enough for it."

"I quit, remember. I enrolled in college today. I put all my savings into tuition."

"So? You can do both. You'll figure it out. Oh, Eva. My dreams are coming true."

Her aunt's dreams might be coming true. But Eva's were now dashed. How was she going to pay for this apartment, put food on the table, and go to school? And with the semester starting next week, she couldn't get a refund. She was screwed.

Chapter Five

Fran walked into the room inside the church. It was a Sunday school classroom but the boys and girls inside weren't toddlers. Though they sure were acting like infants.

Boys with sagging pants, even though they wore belts, sat on desks making overtures to young girls who wore more makeup than grown women and small shirts that were meant for five-year-olds.

They were out of their seats or half in their seats. The seats were not in lined up rows. One kid had his shoes unlaced as he swaggered amongst the crowd. The disorder gave Fran a headache.

Even worse, they were all talking over one another. One kid was blaring loud music from his earbuds. That couldn't be safe. This had to stop.

Fran took a deep breath and in his most commanding voice, called the madness to a halt. "Ah-ten-tion!"

All action ceased. All eyes went to him.

"Kindly take your seats."

All of the girls did as they were told, finding seats for their barely covered rumps. About half of the boys followed suit. A few hesitated. One defiantly stood his ground. It was the unlaced kid.

"Who are you to tell us what to do?" The kid swaggered up to Fran. His pants sagged enough to show off his dingy underwear. He stopped short of coming within grasping distance.

Fran closed that distance with two long strides. "Corporal Francisco DeMonti. Are you in the right place, son?"

Though there was no verbal threat in his words,

Fran made sure the menace in his voice was loud and clear. He knew he shouldn't get himself this worked up. But his heart rate hadn't increased for fear of this kid. It increased because he saw himself in this kid.

A little punk wanting to prove his manhood, but unsure how. Wanting to puff up his chest, but not having any hairs on his chest yet. Having an increasing ego that could be popped with the wrong prick.

Fran didn't want to deflate the kid. Just bring him down to the size he still needed to be. Not a little kid. Not a grown man. Just a young man.

"Because if you are in the right place," Fran said, "then you might be able to help me out."

The kid chewed at the side of his lip. Fran caught the flicker of relief in the kid's eyes that he wouldn't have to go toe to toe with this bigger man against whom he was obviously outmatched. But still, the kid held his ground, not backing down in the light of authority.

That was unlike Fran in his youth. When a recruiter had come to his high school, Fran recognized the command and took the direction. Not this kid.

"What do you need help with, sir?"

Fran peered over the unlaced kids head to another kid. That kid was notably smaller than the others. Fran couldn't tell if he was younger. There was a mature fire about the kid like those brown eyes had seen more of life than a kid should. But unlike the bigger kids, there was still a light in that kid's gaze.

"I'm supposed to give a speech in this room, but the chairs are out of order. I was hoping to make a circle so I could see everyone's faces and they could see mine. Do you think you could get everyone to make a circle for me?"

"Sure. I can do that."

Fran stood back while the kid got everyone up and out of their seats to form the circle. It wasn't a perfect circle, but it accomplished what he'd set out to do. With the attention off him, the unlaced kid slunk into a seat between other sagging butts. Once the brown-eyed kid was finished and everyone seated, he turned back to Fran.

"This good?"

"Yeah, this is great. Thanks for that ...?" Fran held out his hand while he waited for the kid to offer up his name.

"Carlos."

"Thanks, Carlos. You've got some leadership

skills. That's what I'm here to talk with you all about. Leadership."

Carlos took his seat and gave Fran his attention. The other kids followed suit. Most of them. Unlaced kept his gaze on his shoes.

"Life will eat you up alive if you don't have a plan," Fran began. "Even with a plan, you have to be alert. Don't do anything without honor. Honor brings you loyalty. Loyal people will follow you. I've heard there's been some gang activity in this neighborhood?"

Fran looked around. A few of the boys averted their gazes.

"Isn't a gang like the army?" said Unlaced. "They have a plan. You have to be loyal to get in."

Fran didn't immediately cut the boy off. He nodded, while he thought over the logic. "You make some good points. But dig deeper. What is the plan of the gang?"

"To get money," said another kid. "To protect the neighborhood."

Again, Fran nodded. "But who are the gang members getting money from? Usually, someone who is weaker."

The group of boys, who Fran now noted were wearing the same colors, had no come back for that.

"A real man, or woman, doesn't prey on the weak. In the military, we protect this whole country from those that would try to do us harm. We reach out and help our friends when they are being bullied. That brings honor. To ourselves, to our families, to our community, to our country."

"Are you here to get us to join the military?" asked Carlos.

Fran shrugged. "It's an option. I'm here to make sure you know the difference between someone having your back because of loyalty and someone standing behind you because they're using you."

Carlos's gaze went thoughtful. It was clear he was taking in Fran's words, mulling over their meaning. Meanwhile, the saggy gang huddled in on themselves, closing off anyone on the outside.

That was pretty much the end of Fran's big speech. After a brief silence, he took questions. All anyone wanted to know about was his time in duty, if he'd killed anyone, if he'd fired a gun.

Fran kept the conversation tame. He noted a few of the boys leaning in with keen interest. Carlos was one of those few.

When Fran's time was up, Carlos lingered behind as the others filed out to hear another presentation, or in the case of the gang of boys, leave. Fran's chest swelled with pride that he was able to get through to at least one kid.

"You know what you said in there was nice and all ..." Carlos began.

Fran frowned as he heard the telltale pause of an oncoming *but*.

"But what if the neighborhood you live in is bad?" said Carlos. "And you don't have the money to get out? The only way to keep your family safe just might be by being in a gang."

"There's always another way. Like education."

"You sound like my sister."

"Your sister sounds smart."

"Yeah, she is. But she's still stuck in that neighborhood, too. Her education hasn't gotten us anywhere good so far."

The struggle on the kid's face was clear to see. He wanted to believe, but reality was too harsh. A kid like him would be a prime candidate for the youth program that Fran and Dylan wanted to start on the ranch. Plans on that program had stalled after the edict that everyone get hitched in order to stay. No time like the present to get it moving again.

"Look," Fran fished in his pocket for a card, "I want you to come out to this ranch. We're starting a program that I think you might be interested in."

The kid shook his head and stepped back from the card. "My family doesn't believe in charity. We work for what we get."

"It's not charity. It's work."

He perked up at that. "Paid work?"

Fran considered that for two seconds. They had the funds between Dylan's inheritance, government grants, and their own monthly pensions. Why not? If Carlos was old enough for a work permit. "Yeah, but there's training you have to go through first. You'll be working with animals. Interested?"

The kid shrugged and lowered his head, but not before Fran saw a light of interest in his eyes. Carlos pocketed the card and headed down the hall in the same direction the little gang had headed.

But Fran was undaunted. Minds didn't change in a matter of minutes. It took time. He'd gotten some of the kids interested in the military. One he was sure he'd corralled. He wanted to get more. He even considered going after the motley crew. He wanted to see the light burn in their eyes as well.

As soon as the thought took root, he dug it up. His leadership days were done. He wouldn't want to have anyone else's life in his hands for the rest of his life.

"It's a great deal of responsibility to have

someone else's life in your hands. That's why you have to have a plan."

The voice came as though from an angel over his shoulder. It was soft, but strong and resonant at the same time. It stirred the hairs at the nape of his neck, urging him to turn and find it.

Fran turned, and there she was ...

"Hand Over His Heart" is available now!
Get your copy today and see how Fran and Eva
find each other and loose their hearts!

ABOUT THE AUTHOR

Shanae Johnson was raised by Saturday Morning cartoons and After School Specials. She still doesn't understand why there isn't a life lesson that ties the issues of the day together just before bedtime. While she's still waiting for the meaning of it all, she writes stories to try and figure it all out. Her books are wholesome and sweet, but her are heroes are hot and heroines are full of sass!

And by the way, the E elongates the A. So it's pronounced Shan-aaaaaaaa. Perfect for a hero to call out across the moors, or up to a balcony, or to blare outside her window on a boombox. If you hear him calling her name, please send him her way!

ALSO BY SHANAE JOHNSON

The Brides of Purple Heart

On His Bended Knee

Hand Over His Heart

Offering His Arm

His Permanent Scar

Having His Back

You can sign up for Shanae's Reader Group at

http://bit.ly/PurpleHeartBrides